# INDIAN AMBUSH?

Spur lay on his back, then leaned up on his elbows a moment to check his mare. She was moving around as if something was bothering her.

Suddenly something flashed in front of his eyes and he felt the cold steel of a knife blade pressing against his throat. Spur tensed. The knife was poised to slash across his windpipe. He was totally at the mercy of his unknown assailant.

Spur felt movement behind him, and heard a soft sound that wasn't a word.

"I'm just passing through. I won't harm your lands. I'm not a scout for the army. I come in peace," he said.

As quickly as it came, the knife was removed from his throat and he heard a laugh behind him, feminine laughter that trailed off as he sat up and spun around, his hand clawing for the gun at his side.

"Colonel McCoy, you won't need your weapon. I won't hurt you—I came to help you."

He couldn't see through the murky darkness, but he recognized the voice. It was the pretty little Indian girl he'd met at the fort. Now it was Spur's turn to laugh. "Chitsa, welcome to Dakota Territory!"

# Also in the SPUR Series by Dirk Fletcher

# SPUR

## INDIAN MAID

### Dirk Fletcher

LEISURE BOOKS ∞ NEW YORK CITY

A LEISURE BOOK

Published by

Dorchester Publishing Co., Inc.
41 E. 60 St.
New York City

Copyright © 1984 by Dirk Fletcher

Printed in the United States of America

# CHAPTER ONE

*May 12, 1870—Northwestern Nebraska.*

*(Everyone on the East coast was talking about the marvels of the Atlantic City Boardwalk finished in June of 1870. Most of the panic caused by the attempt to corner the gold market in September of 1869 had faded. The first Negro U.S. Congressman, J. R. Rainey, was sworn into office. Philadelphia was the scene of a motion picture showing, animated photographic picture projection before a theatre audience. In that same year, the first U.S. Weather Bureau was authorized and the first trademark registered by the government. This was the year the donkey was first used as a symbol for the Democratic party in a cartoon in New York City. The first Japanese legation was established in Washington D.C. and an ambassador arrived. General Phil Sheridan had taken command of the enormous army Division of Missouri. It covered twelve states and three territories,*

*more than a million square miles of land and contained some 192,000 settlers. There were seventy-six established army posts and some 17,000 army regulars under General Sheridan's command. And Spur McCoy was riding from Sidney, Nebraska north to Camp Sheridan near the Dakota Territory line.)*

Spur McCoy sat on his bay behind a light screening of cottonwood brush as he watched the approaching riders with a growing sense of dread: he had been correct. The ponies had no saddles, and the party consisted of two Indians and a white woman who had been tied to her mount.

Spur slid to the ground silently, pulling the sturdy, reliable Spencer repeating carbine from the scabbard. The carbine was only 43 inches long but could fire seven shots as fast as a man could work the trigger guard lever and cock the hammer. The big .56 caliber round was a little short on distance and stopping power, but at close range it could tear off a man's head, white or Indian.

Spur ran quickly to the fringe of rocks thirty yards from the gully. The trio continued along the dry creek as Spur figured they would. They were moving south and west through this hot and unusually dry day in May. They would follow the water course well past his position.

Both Indian braves rode as if half sleeping. Their heads hung down, one hand holding the rawhide hackamore around their ponies' heads as they swayed from time to time on the horses' backs.

The woman wore no hat and had been stripped to the waist, her only garment a green gingham skirt.

6

Her breasts jolted with each step of the pony which had been tethered to the warrior's horse in front. As the trio came closer Spur could see that the woman had been in the sun too long. Her face, shoulders and breasts were badly sunburned, and he could see tears streaking her dust-covered face. Spur knew about Indians' treatment of white women. He made sure there was a round in the Spencer's chamber, then cocked the carbine and rested it over the rock. Spur had no qualms about "fair play" or warning the savages. They were kidnapping the woman; she was tied and a captive. It was his duty to rescue her any way he could.

Spur waited until the trio was exactly opposite him, less than fifty feet away, and at a place where the braves would have few places to hide. He sighted in with the Spencer. He had checked this weapon for accuracy the day before against a giant cottonwood, firing at a carved X. It had fired a hair high and to the right at 100 yards.

Spur sighted down on the first Indian's head, aiming slightly above his ear and to the left. He squeezed slowly and when the Spencer fired, the bullet tore through the redskin's ear, exploding out his forehead, splattering brain matter, bone chips, and blood and gore all over the dusty trail. The dead Indian jolted from the saddle and sprawled in the dust. His horse stopped.

Spur pulled back on the trigger guard at once, cocked the carbine and swung the muzzle to the second Indian. In the three seconds the movements took Spur, the remaining Indian had tumbled off his horse on the side away from Spur and raced toward a pile of rocks using his horse as a shield. Spur fired twice more, and saw one round slam through the Indian's leg and send him tumbling, but by then the savage was protected by the rocks where there was plenty of cover to hide his retreat.

Spur looked at the woman. She sat on the horse, and started at the sound of his weapon, shaking her head in numb surprise. Her horse had shied away at the smell of death, then quieted, glad to stand still for any reason.

Spur left his concealment and ran to the woman, cut the rawhide binding her to the horse and helped her down. He led her to the shade of the cottonwoods, and gave her a drink from his canteen.

. For a moment he wondered if she were out of her mind. She sat there nude to the waist and either not conscious of the fact or not disturbed whatsoever by it, he couldn't tell which. Her long blonde hair was tangled and dirty, her shoulders, back, breasts, stomach and face all burned a bright angry red, but not blistered by the relentless May Nebraska sun. He guessed she had not been a captive for very long. Spur pulled open the carpet bag on his pack horse, took out one of his lightweight cotton shirts and found a large kerchief. He laid them in front of the woman who stared at them, then looked up at him without a word.

She had the largest, most interesting eyes he had ever seen. They were light brown, with flecks of gold, and so wide and wondering that she looked like a lost fawn. Her oval face was unmarked by time or toil and he guessed she was no more than twenty-three. She was a foot shorter than Spur, and couldn't weigh a hundred pounds. Her breasts were full and high with small budlike nipples centered in dark pink areolas.

"Oh, my," she said at last, her voice strained, but pleasant. She glanced up at him with a kind of bewildered gaiety. "It's so hot out today, I'm just totally bemused."

"Yes, Ma'am, it certainly is hot. I brought a shirt for you."

She stared at the shirt, took it when he gave it to her, but made no effort to put it on. Spur slid the shirt around her shoulders, helped her push her arms into the sleeves and rolled up the cuffs so her hands showed. He waited another moment, then, since she seemed incapable of helping herself, buttoned the front. McCoy folded the kerchief into a triangle and fastened it over her head, tying it under her chin. He realized she was barefoot, a standard Indian tactic for captives so they wouldn't try to run away.

She watched him, her face working, as though she were waking from a deep sleep.

"Thank you," she said slowly as if searching for words.

"You're welcome." He waited a moment, then gave her another drink from his canteen, making sure she didn't take too much. She looked down at the shirt she wore and a smile touched her lips, then faded away.

"Would they have killed me?" she asked in a voice so devoid of emotion that it made Spur uneasy.

"Yes—later."

"Oh, I see, after they. . . ."

"We should be moving away from here. There

could be more Indians about."

"No," she said positively. "They were alone, a raiding party. Sioux. I saw them kill a rancher and his wife."

Spur had heard about the fighting qualities of the Sioux, fierce plains Indians who were battling to save their homeland. He'd heard they were, next to the Apaches, the most fierce fighters.

"Are you from the army at Camp Sheridan?"

She didn't answer for a moment, then she raised huge brown eyes filled with tears.

"I was . . . once."

"How long have you been with the Indians?"

"Two days. I can't ever go back to Camp Sheridan."

"Of course you can. That's where I'm headed. It can't be more than a day's ride north."

"I can't go back!" She looked down at the shirt again. "Oh. . . ." She stared at him. "This must be your shirt. I must have been. . . . Yes—they made me take off my blouse and chemise. I . . ." Tears flooded her eyes again.

"I understand. My name is Colonel Spur McCoy. I'm with the Quartermaster Corps, requisition and supply. I'm out here on a survey. Are you—is your husband in the army?"

She wiped away the tears. "Yes, at Camp Sheridan. That's why I can't go back."

"You can go back with me." Spur smiled and pointed to the north. "We really should be moving. Can you ride? We'll ride double on my bay. She's sturdy and you don't look like you weigh that much."

The sun went under a cloud and he saw her getting

herself emotionally ready for what lay ahead. He knew why she felt she couldn't go back. She had been captured by Indians, most surely violated several times in those two days. The other wives would shun her. If she were an officer's wife her husband would be in an intolerable situation and undoubtedly would ask for a transfer. If he were an enlisted man, it might be easier, but the women would be more outwardly vicious.

Spur found two pair of heavy socks and used them to make temporary footgear for her, then helped her mount the bay and they rode away. At first she barely touched him, riding behind, then at last she put her arms around him and sobbed against his back.

"I'm sorry," she said once, her voice breaking.

Spur turned to look at her swollen, red, beautiful eyes.

"Ma'am, you've been through an ordeal in hell that no one should have to withstand, and you've survived. I reckon you're strong enough to stand up to those cats back at the camp. You're alive, and not injured, that's the important part."

She held him tightly a moment with her arms, her head still resting against his back. "I wish other men thought the way you do," she whispered, then she sobbed again. Spur could think of nothing to say to make her feel better.

All afternoon the sun came in and out from behind the clouds, and the day cooled. There was a hint of rain in the air. About five o'clock Spur selected a sheltered spot near a small stream, a thicket of willow and a few wild mulberry bushes and some wild plum. He stopped in the shade.

"I'm not sure how much farther it is to Camp Sheridan. If it's all right with you, we'll make camp here and let you rest up before going on in tomorrow."

"Another night to account for," she said softly.

"You don't have to account for anything to anyone," Spur said, angry but not at her. "Your husband will be overjoyed to have you back safe and well."

She laughed bitterly and it so surprised Spur that he turned and gawked at her. She stopped and took a long deep breath.

"You don't know my husband. And you *certainly* don't know army wives." Her attitude changed then; seemingly her resolve strengthened and her spirits rose.

"Yes, Colonel McCoy, let's stop here. It will be a blessing to be able to sleep without being tied up."

They halted and Spur unpacked his light camping outfit, a small two-man army tent four feet high at the center, three army blankets, and his mess gear. He set up the tent and spread out two of the army blankets as a ground cover, and told her the tent was hers. Then he started a fire before dusk closed in, and cooked some of his provisions. First he fried the rest of his bacon, then sliced fresh potatoes into the drippings and mixed in diced onions.

Spur boiled coffee and sliced a loaf of brown bread from his pack. The woman had stayed in the tent while he cooked. Only when he told her the food was ready did she come out. He had provided her with a basin of water, soap, comb and a towel and she had made an attempt to look presentable. Now her face was scrubbed and her hair clean and combed.

She came out of the tent with the tails of his long shirt tied in a knot in front. All the buttons but one were fastened below her chin. She sat down on the log and watched Spur.

"Colonell McCoy, my name is Janet Casselberry—Mrs. Robert First Lieutenant Casselberry."

Spur gave a short bow and handed her a tin plate with half the fried potatoes, onions and bacon. "It's a pleasure to meet you, Mrs. Casselberry. I'm sure your husband will be proud of you for showing so much courage."

She nodded. "I'm sorry I was so . . . so vague when you rescued me. I think I was a little out of my mind with the heat, the terror, the rage, and the shock of seeing that Indian's head shatter just in front of me." She looked up and in the firelight her eyes were even more beautiful. "I went a little crazy. I didn't even realize that I was—uncovered." She looked away, blushing. "I thank you for saving my life, at least what is left of it. I realize this isn't a worthy show of gratitude, but that will come later when I am in a better position."

"Mrs. Casselberry, your life is just beginning. You'll always remember this episode, but you will outlive it and defeat it, and be happy and fulfilled. Don't decide anything right now. Wait until we get back to the camp. If your husband doesn't welcome you with open arms, I'll have the scoundrel horse-whipped and then courtmartialed."

Janet smiled at him. It was a delicately beautiful smile. "Colonel, I know you're trying to bolster my spirits. I appreciate that. I'm also intelligent enough to know you can't possibly influence or courtmartial my lieutenant. But I thank you for the

13

thought. Now, where did you learn to make such delicious fried potatoes?" Her plate was empty and the two large slices of bread had vanished as well.

"When did you eat last?" he asked her.

"Eat? I can't remember." She stood and he was surprised at her quickness. "I'll do the dishes. Is there any sand to use to wash things?"

He brought some sand in a pan of water and she washed the plates clean, then the skillet and helped him put them away. They sat beside the small fire not talking, just watching the coals, Spur thinking how glad he was to be out in the wilds again, to smell the crisp air, to hear the cry of the night creatures.

She peered at him a moment, then threw some twigs on the fire so it blazed up and she could see his face plainly.

"Colonel McCoy, I hope you won't try and make the people back at Camp Sheridan accept me. I know how they will react, almost exactly what they will do. It's the army. We were stationed at another army post where a woman was rescued from the Indians. She had been gone almost a year. At last she escaped and was found by a surveying crew. She wasn't army, but she stayed at the fort for two months.

"At first the women only gossiped about her. Everyone said she was used by all the braves in the tribe. Then the story was that she was the prize for the best warrior and was passed from brave to brave. At last they said she was claimed by the second chief as his second wife. Then the women began asking her about what it was like—ah—er . . .

14

you know . . . being with a savage. It got so whenever she came outside she was pounced on by the women and asked embarrassingly outrageous questions. She was never invited to dinner, or to the officers' dances, or to any socials. Two months after she arrived at the post she put a gun to her head and killed herself. I *know* what it's going to be like."

"But with you it's different. You *are* army."

"Yes, and an officer's wife, which will make it twice as bad for me." Her eyes held him and he knew it was true. He had rescued her, only to take her back into another hell.

A short time later they let the fire die down and Spur told her goodnight. He tied the flaps on the tent after she went inside.

"Good night, Colonel, and thank you," she said through the canvas.

"You're entirely welcome, Mrs. Casselberry."

Spur lay down on his blanket, with his favorite Merwin & Hurlburt .44 loaded, cocked and lying under his right hand. The night was warm. He could see the moon edging past some clouds and filtering faint light through the trees. Crickets began chirping as the fire went out; soon the night birds called and Spur dozed, knowing that the world was once again at peace.

Something touched his shoulder. His hand closed around the six-gun and he sat up suddenly, the .44 aiming at the dark, shadowy figure bending over him.

"Colonel! It's me!" Janet Casselberry whispered.

"Oh, sorry." He let the hammer down gently on the loaded chamber. "Are you all right?"

"No. The tent is so stuffy, hot. I've brought out the blankets. Would it bother you if I slept out here?"

"No bother at all."

She nodded and put her blankets beside his. Janet Casselberry looked at him sternly. "I'm not meaning in any way that I want to get intimate . . ."

"I understand."

She smiled into the darkness. "Yes. Yes, Colonel, I really think you do." She lay down, stretched out and turned on her side. They both were still fully clothed. She squirmed a moment, then reached a hand out and touched his shoulder.

"Just so I know you're there," she said. Her voice went softer so he had to strain to hear her. "I was so frightened those two days—I'm still frightened. I don't want to be alone."

He didn't reply. A moment later she sighed, then almost at once she was breathing deeply, evenly. Janet was sleeping. Spur dozed and woke, dozed again and when he woke the next time, Janet Casselberry was curled against him, her arm over his chest, her head cuddled on his shoulder, as she slept soundly.

Spur wondered about her, worried about what kind of man her husband might be, and at last drifted off to sleep.

# CHAPTER TWO

Fragments of daylight on the eastern horizon awakened Spur several hours later. He opened his eyes without moving, aware of a soft, curved body next to his. Blonde hair tickled his cheek, making him smile. The woman lay half on her side, half against him, her arm over his chest gripping his far side, her legs pressed against his.

Carefully he moved her arm and edged away from her. She slept on. He slid across the blanket, covered her shoulders with one of her blankets and got to his feet quietly. She'd need all the rest she could get to prepare for the hard day coming.

Spur found wood and silently built a cooking fire, then made coffee.

Spur McCoy was thirty-two years old, over six feet tall, and carried two hundred pounds sleekly. He had sandy red hair, a full moustache and mutton chop sideburns. He had strong hands, was an excellent horseman, and a crack shot with derringer, six-gun or rifle. He looked back at the sleeping woman.

She would be off his hands soon and someone else's problem.

For a moment he thought about his assignment. "An inspection survey," he had told her. In a way it was true. And he had once been in the army, though not as a colonel. He had made captain during the Civil War before Lee surrendered. After two years in the army he'd gone to Washington as an aide to Senator Arthur B. Walton, a longtime family friend. In 1865, Charles Spur McCoy was appointed one of the first U.S. Secret Service Agents. Since the Secret Service was the only federal law enforcement agency in existence, it handled a wide range of problems, most of them far removed from the original task of preventing the circulation of counterfeit currency.

He had served six months in the Washington Secret Service office, then was transferred to head the base in St. Louis and handle all problems west of the Mississippi. Spur had been chosen from twenty men for the position because of his excellent marksmanship. He also was the best horseman in the group.

Spur pushed more sticks into the fire. If his Harvard professors could see him now they would be amused. This certainly wasn't the future he had planned. His father was a well-known merchant in New York City and Spur had gone to Harvard as a matter of course, graduating in the class of 1858. Now here he was in the middle of the western Nebraska wilderness heading for an army camp near the Black Hills in Dakota territory. Indians in that area had been acquiring more and more rifles, and the army commander in Chicago wanted to find out their source of supply and have that source eliminated.

William Wood, Spur's Agency director in Washington, had given the assignment to Gen. Wil Halleck, who had passed it on to Spur; since it fell within his jurisdiction.

Spur had taken the train to Sidney, Nebraska, then picked up some gear and headed on horseback nearly 150 miles north to his target.

"You should have wakened me." The sharp, accusing voice cut through his thoughts, and Spur looked over to see Janet sitting up in the blankets. Her blonde hair was rumpled and she still looked half asleep. Two of the buttons on the shirt had come undone during the night and the swell of one breast was tantalizingly revealed. She looked so vulnerable, so alone and appealing that Spur had to stifle a surge of desire.

"Good morning. I figured the rest would do you good."

"For my coming ordeal no doubt?" She stood, briskly fastened the two shirt buttons then knelt down and began straightening and folding the blankets. "Aren't you in a rush to get started?"

"No."

"Oh?" It surprised her. She sat back on her heels and looked at him. "Well, I am. I want to get it over with. I want to find out what Neil is going to say to me. The suspense is driving me mad!"

Spur grinned. "Anything you say. Coffee?" She nodded and hurried toward him. He could see her breasts bouncing under the shirt and he remembered how beautiful they had been unemcumbered, swaying and swinging free, naked and sunburned . . .

Spur shook his head to clear it and poured a cup of coffee for her. Her fingers touched his as she took it and she glanced up at him quickly, then away.

"Thank you, Colonel."

"My pleasure, Ma'am."

He tried to make small talk about the army post, but she was anxious to be moving. They packed up and she let him help her up on the back of his bay, then he swung up. The pack horse was tethered to his saddle and trailed behind with a slack line.

"Have you any idea how much farther it is to the camp?" he asked her.

She stared around, frowning, and when they came to a slight rise, she murmured, "Yes, I remember that bluff over there. If we angle toward it, we should come to the White River. From here I'd say the camp is upstream about fifteen miles more."

"Thanks. I could use you as my scout."

"I'd probably get us lost."

She put her hands on his shoulders now. Spur found her touch a little unsettling because he kept remembering her large, sunburned breasts and the way they bounced and swung when she walked. Spur grinned ruefully and kicked the bay into motion. Her arms stole around his waist and he heard her give a small sigh.

By noon they could see the army post nestled beside the White River, an odd collection of log structures chinked with a mixture of mud, sand and lime. There was no outer wall, no palisade to hide behind. The buildings were built against one another in a rough square. As they came closer, Spur saw that the two largest buildings were made of adobe blocks. Like most army buildings of the day, these had been built with whatever materials were close at hand.

When they were barely a mile from the camp, a rider approached them from an angle. The trooper was obviously a lookout of some kind, keeping an eye peeled for anyone who happened to approach the area.

The trooper in his blue uniform and low crowned brown campaign hat rode up, stared at the riders for an astonished moment and saluted.

"Mrs. Casselberry, Ma'am! Glory! We never expected to see you again, Ma'am!"

"Corporal Jeffers, isn't it? I'm quite all right, as you can see. But please don't spread the word. I want my arrival to be a surprise. You may return to your post."

"Yes, Ma'am."

"This is Colonel McCoy, Corporal. He'll be staying at Camp Sheridan for a time."

The corporal stiffened and saluted. Spur returned the salute.

"At ease, Corporal. You're excused to return to your post."

"Yes sir!" the corporal said, saluted again, pulled his horse around and rode hard away from them.

Janet tensed and he felt it. "We better go now, quickly, Colonel McCoy, or I might just get off this horse and start running the other way. My bravado is starting to desert me."

Spur turned and looked her in the eye. "Janet Casselberry, you suffered at the hands of the Sioux and you got away. Those biddies at the camp are not going to be half as tough. Remember that, and you'll do just fine."

A half hour later they created a sensation when they rode through a gate in the fence near the sutler's store. Women streamed from a dozen houses and rushed up to greet Janet, escorting her into her own house. Spur continued to the commanding officer's quarters and tied up his horses.

One room of the commander's residence was partitioned off to form an office. In this separate "office" he conducted the business of the camp.

Spur was asked by a sergeant to wait a moment while the trooper went through a door into the residence section. He came back a moment later with a tall, thin man whose uniform hung on him like rags on a fencepost. Black, thinning hair barely covered an oversized head that seemed too large and heavy for the slender neck. The man's eyes were piercing and black. He made no pretense of cordiality and offered no welcome.

"Colonel? Colonel? I made no request for any kind of a damn survey! What do you mean, survey? Where are your papers?"

Spur picked up a leather case and opened it, handing the lieutenant colonel a sheaf of formal army orders, instructions, and a carte blanche that permitted the bearer to do virtually anything on the post that wasn't overtly seditious or mutinous.

"Yeah, seen this trash before. Killing the goddamned Indians is our job, not mollycoddling some paper shuffler from Washington!" The camp commander sat in a chair behind his desk and peered balefully at Spur who had seated himself in the only other chair in the room.

"I seen this kind of orders during the war. Wrote

up a few myself. Always did it this way when I sent in a horsewhipping spy to get to the bottom of some trouble in an outfit. Ain't no trouble here. No sir, young feller. Don't care if you *are* a full colonel, I got the years and experience on you. Hell, don't matter none! You just keep outa my way, don't make trouble, and I won't give you any problems.''

Spur stood and walked to the desk, frowning down at the older man, who looked up with a touch of impatience.

"Colonel, thank you for introducing yourself. You sound like a man who doesn't really want to stay in the army, or stay in command of this facility. Now what is your name, your permanent rank, and your official mission in this god-forsaken rat's nest?''

The man behind the desk snapped to attention.

"Sir! My name is Ezekiel Underhill. Permanent rank of Major. Brevet Lieutenant Colonel March 1869. Sir! My mission at this post is to render all possible aid to settlers, to maintain the peace with the indignous Indian population, and to follow those army orders issued to me by The Division of Missouri, General Phil Sheridan, commanding.''

"In that case, Colonel, you're doing a damn poor job!''

Lt. Colonel Underhill's face turned red and he started to say something but Spur cut him off with a quick gesture.

"I usually don't use my rank, Underhill. I'd rather work incognito. But in this case I can and I will, if you force me to.''

Colonel Underhill's eyes blazed but his voice was steady.

"Yes, sir. I understand, sir.''

"I hope you do. I'll need quarters, a mount on call, and I don't want an aide trailing me around."

"Yes, sir."

"I'll want to meet all of your officers as soon as possible. Do you have a central mess?"

"No, sir, but we have a social and card party scheduled for tonight, eight sharp. You're welcome to attend."

"Thank you, Colonel Underhill. You're more than kind. Now, if you'll have someone show me to my quarters and provide some hot water, I could use a bath."

An hour later Spur McCoy had finished scrubbing his long body and washing the trail dust out of his hair. He was just about to get out of the tub, when the rear door to his quarters opened and the rounded backside of a woman pushed through the door.

"Don't pay me no attention, Colonel. I'm Molly what is sent over to do up your bed." As she finished speaking, she turned and saw Spur sitting folded up in the oval galvanized wash tub and she giggled. "Lordy, lordy, lordy, now that's what I calls one big tall chunk of mankind!" She dropped the sheets she carried and picked up his towel.

"Now, I wash backs too. Your back all scrubbed clean?"

"Sorry to say it is, Molly."

She laughed and walked around the tub, looking admiringly at his genitals. "My, my! Now *that* is a big one, and I bet he can get one hell of a lot bigger."

Spur chuckled. "No bet, Molly."

"Colonel, I got me this little itch. I mean, if you could help me I'd be ever so grateful."

24

"Itch?"

Molly unbuttoned the top of her blouse and a moment later flipped out a big breast. Molly was decidedly buxom, with short brown hair, a happy chunk who was proud of her rounded figure and billowing breasts. Spur stood, took the towel from her hands and dried himself. She watched in surprised delight as he dried his crotch first and his manhood came up stiff and ready.

"Lord love a duck, I think Mr. Dick there likes me tittie!"

"He loves both of them," Spur said and took three long steps to the rear door and locked it. Molly hurried to the front door and bolted it, then met him by the bed.

"Molly, little darling, do you have another bouncer like that one?" Spur moved his hand around her exposed breast, caressing it gently. It was as large as half a watermelon.

"Hot damn!" Molly said softly. "This is gonna be fun!"

She ran ahead of him to the bed, flopped on it, and spread-eagled herself on the blanket.

Spur sat down on the edge of the bed and she lifted up beside him and reached for his ramrod hard stiff.

"Lordy, lordy, what a prick!" She touched it reverently, then her hand wrapped around and she stroked him twice. Molly bent and kissed the very tip of the purple head and Spur felt a stabbing jolt of desire throughout his body. He pulled her up and took off her blouse and a thin chemise. Both breasts billowed out and Spur groaned in delight as he pushed his face between them, kissing them in turn, working around until he found a heavy brown nipple which he kissed and then nibbled until Molly yelped with pleasure.

"My, my, you *are* an eager fella! I love it! I bet you could just chew my titties off if you wanted to. But I've got places even better!" She wiggled out of her skirt and two petticoats and lay there, round and frankly fat and loving it. She laughed. "Hey, bet you ain't never fucked a real fat girl before. Shit, we're *fun.* We got to be. More bounce to the ounce and we shake like jelly. We have the padding to make your ride more fun." She nodded. "Yeah, I can see you just ain't never fucked a fat girl. Don't worry, time comes, I'll pee a little bit to give you a good target." She set off in shrieking laughter and he put his hand over her mouth to quiet the sound.

"Oh, yeah, I ain't home now." She bounced up and sat beside him again, then grabbed his heavy scrotum and brushed his big balls together tenderly. "Oh, yeah, I got to see what these sweethearts produce. About six times a night I'd say. Christ, wouldn't *that* be a ride!"

She played with him and stroked him a few more times. "Lordy, am I going to eat you! Gonna get down and spread your legs and kiss your big balls, then I'm gonna get each one in my mouth and chew them until you go wild. I can make a fella come just chewing on his nuts, you know that? True. You'll love every hour of it." She laughed. "Course, I can't stay no hour. Got to be back in about twenty minutes. You a quick performer?"

She turned and went down on his staff, gulping more of it in her mouth than Spur thought possible, then began a rhythmical bobbing of her head that soon produced urgent results. Spur caught her head and pulled her up.

"Now, darlin'," he said, "we better make it now or it ain't got time to happen." She spread herself out on the bed and lifted her knees. Spur knew exactly what to do next. A moment later they were locked together and she pushed her legs higher on his sides but couldn't lock them on top.

Spur's steam pressure had been building since the moment she had pushed in through the back door of his room and turned around. Now he stroked quickly and before he knew it the magic trigger tripped and he was off on a mission of no return. A moment later, it was over. and he lay on top of her panting as if he would never get enough oxygen back into his depleted system.

She hugged him tightly, not letting him lift away when he attempted to.

"Lordy, but you were good! I had my own party and you didn't even feel me, you was way out there in the sky somewhere. I even talked to you, but nothing would make you hear. You is something, Colonel. Damn! You're really a wild one."

Spur moved away and sat up. She might be a good source of information. He'd try a little gentle questioning.

"Molly, you know this camp. What do you think about Colonel Underhill? Is he a good soldier?"

"Shit, no! He's half crazy. He goes on tears now and then and the men don't know what he wants or how they should do something. He changes his ass for his nose more times than you can piss in a circle. He's just plain crazy, but nobody can get him relieved. Major Rutherford—Vern. Now *there* is a good man. He's fair and honest, fucking good soldier, but he's stuck under Underhill. Damn shame. One of these days this camp is gonna blow sky high, and when things come down, Underhill won't be here. He's an Injun hater like all officers. Christ, us enlisted can get along with or without the savages. Figure they got a right to live too, and this is their land we're on. But they pulled back into the hills, and now pretty soon orders will come to push them back farther. Been happening for a hundred and fifty years now, longer than that I guess."

She sat up and began collecting her clothes. "Christ, I got to get moving. Got two more beds to make up. I work the Bachelor Officers' Quarters. Get paid three dollars a fucking week for it, so me and my man make out fine." She grinned in reply to Spur's unanswered question. "Naw, hell, he don't mind my fucking around a little. Just so I don't bring home none of them diseases. He's been to Alaska. Says the Eskimoes got it right, fucking a cunt can't hurt it none, just makes it better." She laughed. "So far I think them Eskies is right!"

She dressed quickly, picked up the sheets she had dropped and hurried out the back door.

Spur dressed in clean clothes, civilian blue shirt and pants and a wide belt with a silver buckle. He was looking forward to the bachelor officers' mess call at five o'clock.

# CHAPTER THREE

The Officers' Mess was adjacent to the kitchen, on the far side from the enlisted men's messhall, but much smaller. Most of the officers had family with them, since this was not designated as a dangerous or hardship post. Only five officers ate at the mess that night, plus one civilian who was introduced as an army scout, on the army payroll but due soon to come to the end of his contract.

The highest ranking man there was Captain Grove, the camp adjutant. He was a quiet little man, barely five-feet two, who had little to say and did not enter into the round of jokes. The most talkative was the most recent arrival, Lt. Omer Imhoff, who had been at the camp for six months. He was a newly commissioned officer, fresh out of West Point, and had waited only three months for a post. Most freshly graduated second lieutenants from West Point had up to a year's wait before they received their actual commission and were appointed to an army post or camp.

"Of course I was damn lucky to get this spot. I'd have taken anything. But this senator in Washington said he could get me a post if I would contribute a hundred dollars to his campaign fund. What the hell, I borrowed the money from my mother, paid him and here I am."

Imhoff was solidly built, about five-feet ten, and probably weighed over two hundred pounds. But there was no obvious flab; he looked all muscle and willing to use it. He was blond, with a fair moustache and a short trimmed beard of a slightly darker shade. He was the most friendly of the group. Everyone knew who Spur was and why he was there —the quartermaster survey story.

"How did you get to be a colonel so fast in Quartermaster?" Lt. Imhoff asked.

"I must know that same senator you do, Lieutenant," Spur shot back. Everyone laughed.

"Are we still at a standstill on cleaning out the savages in the Black Hills?" one of the officers asked.

"You must realize I don't get into the operational side of the decision making," Spur began. "But from what I hear the official position is that we have a treaty with the Sioux. Unless they break it we are honor bound to respect their lands."

"But when the murdering bastards break out and kill and loot our settlers and farmers and then run back into the Sioux lands, we can't go in after them?" another officer demanded.

"Well, now, gentlemen, the army has always been rather firm about that. A hostile is a hostile, and if he's broken the law or a treaty, the army usually goes in and gets him."

"Yeah, the only safe Indian is a scalped Indian," Imhoff said.

Captain Grove shook his head. "I heard it the only good Indian is a dead one."

"At least old two-gun Sheridan is going to have his way with the Military Division of the Missouri," Imhoff said. "Ten will get you a hundred that we're on full-scale hunt-down-and-kill Indian missions by the end of the year. General Sheridan is sitting back there in Omaha dancing with every pretty skirt he sees and wishing he could be out here killing Indians."

Lt. Wes Pauley grinned and pounded the table with his fist. "Yes, and it's about time! I've seen enough innocent settlers killed, and wagon trains wiped out! I just don't believe in molly-coddling these savages. The only way we'll have peace with them is to grind them down and wipe them out if necessary." Lt. Pauley was slight and was never seen without his service revolver. He had mouse-brown hair and a straggling moustache; otherwise he was clean shaven.

The main course came at last and the men settled down to eating.

Spur sat beside the only other civilian at the table, who said he was Buffalo Kane, the post scout. He was long haired, with a full beard, both unkempt, and wore a fringed buckskin shirt that Spur knew was far too hot for the weather; but he evidently refused to part with it. He had on regulation blue pants and army boots. Spur had felt Buffalo Kane stiffen when Lt. Pauley talked about wiping out all Indians. But when Spur looked over at him, the scout was working on a slab of roast beef with a

31

vengeance, cutting and eating, and lifting his laden fork to his mouth with his left hand.

The talk turned to the army, about other commands, other posts, and when the dessert of deep-dish wild plum pie was gone, the men began drifting away. When Spur said good night to the others, they reminded him about the card party and social at eight o'clock.

"Then you'll have a chance to meet some of the illustrious ladies of the post," Lt. Imhoff said. He laughed. "Of course some of the most important females won't be there because they're only wives of enlisted men. But some of the officers here think those ladies have abundant charms!" The officers all laughed and the men ambled away into the dusk.

Outside, the scout called to Spur.

"Colonel, could I talk to you a bit?"

Spur nodded and they leaned against the wall of the sutler's store which was closed and dark.

"I got to talk to you, Colonel," Buffalo Kane said earnestly. "I got me something that's eating my guts to pieces and it's gettin' worse and worse. Nobody in camp will listen to me. My contract is up in a month, and I got to settle it quick."

Spur nodded, wishing he could light up one of his favorite crooked black cigars, but they were all in his quarters.

"Just what is this problem, Kane?"

"My family, sir. While I was on a patrol up near the Black Hills, somebody murdered my whole family, my wife and my two sons. The boys was only three and four. Just butchered them. And nobody will help me find out who did it. But I got my suspicions, and I think the murderers are right here at Camp."

Spur had been listening with half an ear, still evaluating the officers he had met, but now his interest quickened.

"My wife, Walking Fawn, was only twenty. She was Cheyenne—that's why we weren't allowed to live here at the camp. I built a nice little place two miles downstream. Not fancy, but Walking Fawn thought it was beautiful. I been a scout a long time, Colonel. I know the army, but I never thought they would do this to me."

"You sure it was the army, Mr. Kane?"

"Hell, yes! I'm a scout, a tracker. I put the whole thing together from what I found out there. I came home two days after they were killed. There had been six men, all on army mounts. One man held the horses. They set up in three spots around the shanty. I picked up sixty brass casings at those three spots. They were having target practice, and I won't rest easy in my mind until I see the guilty ones hung, especially the officer who led the patrol. I know who was out with me, and the other officers here. But you got to help me. They stick together like molasses and glue."

"You went to Colonel Underhill?"

"Shit! He threw me out of his office. Said he wouldn't have signed me on as a scout if'n he knew I was a squaw man."

"Major Rutherford?"

"Good man, should be commanding here. He said he can't do anything without the approval of the colonel, and that crazy man is an all-out Indian hater.

33

You just got to help me out somehow!"

"You have any solid proof, Kane?"

"You bet. I found some of my wife's jewelry in the sutler's store. I got his signed paper that says it was sold to him by two soldiers, but he says he don't remember which ones. They was needing some drinking money. And they sold the brooch and pendant and a piece of pounded gold two days after my family was killed." Kane rubbed his rough hand across angry, wet eyes. "You got to help me, Colonel, 'fore I go plumb crazy myself! Don't matter much what happens to me, long as I get at least one of them. The men wouldn't of done it unless an officer ordered them to. Hell, one or two of the men had been down and seen my boys."

"The normal course would be to register a complaint through regular channels. . . ."

"Hell, Colonel, you know that wouldn't work. Anyway, I'm not Army. I don't got to go through no damn channels." He stared up at Spur for a few seconds. "Damn, I don't think you're spit-and-polish either. You can twist some tails, get some action going. Christ, tell old Underhill you know the Inspector General is coming this direction. That might shake him off his damn stubborn stool."

"How long had your family been living here?"

"Almost six months. Most of the men and officers knew all about me and my family. Someplaces things gets touchy, but I thought it was all simmered down here."

"You have this all written out, Kane? I'll need to know the date they were killed, when you went on the patrol, the officers and men with you on the patrol, and which officers were left in camp."

"I . . . I don't write none too good, Colonel. But I got it all writ out by a friend."

Spur said he would look it over and returned to his quarters, where he put on his uniform. He wouldn't wear it much, but he wanted to get off on the right foot with the ladies. In the course of the evening he would meet all the officers on the post. The odds were that the rifles were being supplied to the Indians through this very camp. If so, that would mean an officer would be needed to make the contacts on both sides. Spur would evaluate and check out each officer on the post.

An hour later Spur was on his way to the social at Colonel Underhill's quarters when someone called to him. An officer in full dress uniform hurried up and saluted. Spur returned the salute. He had not met this young lieutenant before.

"Colonel, sir. If I could delay you for a moment there is an urgent matter we must discuss."

In the flickering light of a lamp on a post, Spur could see the rugged, stern, almost angry expression on the young officer's face.

"That might be arranged, Lieutenant, if you will have the courtesy to identify yourself and state your problem."

"Sorry, sir. First Lieutenant Casselberry, Company B. It's about my wife, sir."

Spur nodded and studied the man in the lamplight. He was about two inches under six feet, stocky, clean-shaven, and his face was set in a scowl. His dark eyes were angry, his brow furrowed.

"Yes—Mrs. Casselberry. I hope you welcomed her back warmly. She was a bit concerned."

"I did *not* welcome her back, sir. My relations

with my wife are a private affair, a personal matter, not a subject for casual speculation."

"You're quite right if you go by the book. But the woman was as terrified of you and coming back to the fort as she was of the Indians."

"There were no Indians, Colonel."

"I beg your pardon, Lieutenant? Didn't she tell you?"

"She did. I've ordered her to change her story. *There were no Indians.*"

Spur stared at the officer, unable to believe his ears. At last he nodded. "You're afraid if it is whispered around that she was captured by Indians, it will adversely affect her reputation on this post."

"Sir, I *know* what it would do. I've seen it happen before. That's why I made her carry a hide-out gun. She says she used up all four rounds shooting at the Indians."

"And you would rather that she had . . ."

"Yes, quite right, Colonel. I had ordered her to save the last bullet for herself, if all else failed. I even showed her where to hold the gun, just over her right ear."

Spur shook his head incredulously. "I'm not sure anyone will swallow some trumped-up story, Lieutenant. I suppose you've told her to say that she became lost, disoriented perhaps, and walked the wrong way while picking—what, crabapples? Then, amazingly enough, I found her, untouched and pure as the driven snow."

"Yes, that's close enough, sir."

"But what about *my* story, Lieutenant?"

"Sir, it's my private affair. It seems to me the only way out of an intensely embarrassing situation.

You must see it my way. After all, Colonel, we are both Army."

Spur's first impulse was to lash out and knock the man into the dust beside the sutler's store. Instead, he stared at the blank, tense, stern face of the officer.

"Yes, Lieutenant, we *are* both Army. And every army man I know treats his wife with the utmost respect, consideration, love and tenderness. What does Mrs. Casselberry say about this plan of yours?"

"It doesn't matter what she thinks or says, sir. I am in command of my own household."

"Your most important command is of one wife."

"Yes, sir, if the colonel wishes to put it that way."

"How does she feel about your plan, Lieutenant?"

The young officer hesitated, stared at Spur with controlled anger for a moment, then scowled. "She doesn't like it. Although she knows how the women on the post would treat her, what the other officers would subject me to, she still says we should tell the truth."

"Which is?"

"She was picking choke cherries, strayed too far along the river and was grabbed by a pair of Sioux hunters who obviously didn't know they were so close to any army post. You came upon her the following morning. She swears they didn't touch her, just made her ride stripped to the waist. But if the women find out she was captured by the Sioux. . . . You know what that would mean, Colonel. You know what these army wives can do to a woman with a taint of *any* kind."

"And it might affect your career as well. Isn't

that what's bothering you most, Lieutenant? Are you West Point?"

"Yes, of course."

"Christ! We should burn that place down!"

"Sir!"

Spur's angry glare bored into the younger man. "You know what bothers me the most, Casselberry? Your attitude toward this whole thing. You haven't once mentioned the suffering your wife has been through. You haven't worried about how she is bearing up under it. You haven't been *concerned* about your wife. What you're really worried about is your career."

"Sir, if this gets out, my wife would never be able to hold up her head on any army post. Everyone would say that she had been defiled by the Indians. The women would cackle and gossip and the officers would all ostracize both her and me. I would never be trusted again. Don't you *understand?* This is a frontier post. We fight Indians here. Our womenfolk are instructed, are *ordered* never to allow themselves to be captured alive. Janet knew what to do."

"And now, since she had the audacity and the gall to get rescued and did *not* kill herself, you are outraged."

The man's face froze into a harsh, angry stare. "If the colonel says so, sir."

"Damn, haven't you learned anything since you got out of the Point?"

"Sir, all I'm asking you to do is support me when I tell how you found Janet wandering in the plains along the river. She lost her way, that's all. No harm done. It isn't much to ask."

"Lieutenant, which is more important to you,

your army career or the well-being of your wife?"

"My. . . . Sir, I'm really not sure, not now. But I don't *need* to make a choice between them." He paused and came to rigid attention. "Sir, this is a most difficult favor to ask of a superior officer. It is extremely hard for me. I would appreciate the colonel's answer."

"I'll think about it, Lieutenant Casselberry. If it comes up tonight, you make your explanations, and by then I'll have decided what to do. I'll either support you—or totally ruin your army career. You're dismissed, Lieutenant."

Casselberry shivered, saluted, did an about face and stamped away.

When Spur moved on toward the lieutenant colonel's quarters, he met two more officers and joined them. They all introduced themselves. At the commander's house a receiving line was established with Spur beside Mrs. Underhill, who turned out to be a short, round lady in a pink gown with light blue trim, and an elaborate hairdo with her curls piled on her head and spilling downward. Spur assumed it was the latest style. Her name, it turned out, was Grace.

"Colonel McCoy, we're all so thrilled how you rescued that poor Janet Casselberry. Found her wandering along the river and all. We're so proud of you! It's just pure chance that some roving band of Indians didn't find her first. You know of course what *they* would have done!"

By the time the receiving line was through, eighteen officers and twelve women had come through and chatted with Spur. He had a first impression of each of the officers, and would get a list later with the assignment of each man and any personal information Major Rutherford might be able to come up with.

Soon the card games began. Two couples were playing whist and several more engaged in a game new to Spur called bezique, in which the queen of spades and the jack of diamonds made a large count. Three games of four-handed, serious poker began. Spur drifted from one table to another, and at last settled into a poker game with Major Rutherford. No one was allowed to lose more than five dollars.

"New money, men—the colonel is anxious to make a good impression by losing his stakes quickly," Major Rutherford said. "And since he's a redhead too, watch out for him." Four other officers at the table laughed. The sixth person seated there smiled and twin dimples dented her cheeks. Spur had met her earlier; Felicia Jones, daughter of the camp doctor, Captain Hiram Jones.

Felicia was shuffling the cards. She nodded. "Yes, Colonel, I *do* know how to play poker, and I usually win. I am an excellent bluffer and also I draw marvelous cards, so try your luck. This game will be draw poker, jacks or better to open. The ante is twenty cents. Everyone in?"

Spur smiled, tossed two reds into the pot from the stack of chips he had received for his five dollars, and waited for his cards.

He was sitting beside Major Rutherford, and liked the man at once. He seemed to be a reasonable, calm, efficient man who was at the same time attuned to the needs of his position and the men and officers who served under him. It was completely opposite to the impression Spur had received from Colonel Underhill.

Spur discarded to a pair of eights, bought his cards for a dime and folded. Felicia shot him an approving glance. She won the pot with three kings, and passed the deal along. She looked at Spur again and smiled, then shifted her gaze. She was a delightfully pretty girl, with a flair for dressing well, and from what he had seen so far, a bright, outgoing personality. But if he wanted more than a smile from her, Spur knew he would have to made the advances.

He played poker automatically, trying to remember each face and name at the table. It wasn't his best talent. He concentrated on a few of the men, trying to block out the women for the moment.

Lt. Casselberry had arrived slightly late, apologizing to Mrs. Underhill, who waved him away. He did not seem to be popular with the other officers who were polite, but a bit distant. Spur's secondary impression of him reinforced the previous one: he was a professional soldier, dedicated to the army, good at what he did but as cold and stiff as a military saber. Would he sell army rifles to the Indians? Spur didn't know, not yet.

Among the eighteen officers present, Spur could find no obvious candidate for a suspect. Perhaps any one of them could turn traitor, given the right situation, or a pressing need. But the Army was so righteously anti-Indian that it must be a strange kind of man who would help arm the savages who he would later have to fight. It was grotesque in a way, and Spur wondered if he were dealing with a man who had lost his mind. At the very least, the traitor's understanding of right and wrong must be seriously confused.

The card games broke up promptly at ten o'clock and the dancing began. Felicia Jones played the violin, two men strummed guitars and another played a brightly decorated accordion. The carpet was rolled up and the dancing began. During every other dance set, Spur noticed that Felicia Jones was dancing rather than playing, with a multitude of different partners. Twice he spotted Lt. Omer Imhoff guiding her around. She was the most popular girl in the group, the only unmarried one as far as he knew, and the young bucks were constantly cutting in on each other.

Spur danced with the colonel's lady, and then wandered over and watched the band. In the middle of one number, Felicia smiled, put down her fiddle and came up beside him.

"Could I have the honor of this dance?" she asked with a mischievous smile.

"I would be delighted," Spur said. "In Washington D.C., it's becoming positively fashionable for ladies to ask the gentlemen to dance."

He rested one hand lightly on her waist, took her right hand in his and spun her away in a waltz. She made a contented sound deep in her throat, almost a purr.

"You are an excellent dancer, Colonel McCoy, the best on the post."

"If I'm doing well, it's only because I'm inspired by such a beautiful lady, who is also such an exquisite dancer," Spur said gallantly. He was pleased to see a slight blush tinge her cheeks.

"Thank you," she said, shyly, her bravado suddenly deserting her. "I hope you don't think that I was too forward. The officers' wives are going to be gossiping about me all week!"

"And well they should. They are jealous of the marvelous way you dance. I've waltzed with some of them, and most don't know their right foot from their left."

Felicia laughed. "Goodness, please don't tell *them* that!" The dance ended and Spur took her back to the chair where she had left her instrument.

"Thank you for the dance, Miss Jones, it was delightful."

She bowed slightly, smiled and turned away.

Spur walked across the room and sat at a table near Major Rutherford. Their host had supplied sipping whiskey and most of the men cut it with branch water, but Major Rutherford took his straight in a shot glass. Spur mentioned that he would like to look over the personnel files the next day and the major nodded.

"Yes, I expected you would ask. We have a good group of men here. There are a few I would rather send back to Omaha, but that happens in any command." He watched Spur closely for a moment. "Colonel, have we met before? I served in Washington D.C. for a short time right after the war."

"I was still pushing cavalry in Texas at that time, Major." Spur paused and lowered his voice. "Major, is there some kind of a problem here with your commanding officer?"

Major Rutherford took a long breath, then looked up. "I have not found sufficient justification for anything approaching the evidence needed to relieve anyone of command. All of us have a few little

43

quirks—Zeke just has a few more than most. But as far as going any further, I wouldn't want any part of it, not right now."

"Thanks, Major, forget I mentioned it."

"Gladly."

Lt. Casselberry sat down on the other side of the major and caught his attention.

"Sir, I just wanted to report that my wife is fine, no worse for her experience. It was as we feared. She became lost and disoriented and simply walked the wrong way along the river. She went away from the post instead of toward it. She had discovered her mistake and was on the way back when Colonel McCoy overtook her and gave her a ride to camp. Sir, I hope this will put to rest any of the rumors that I've heard about her being captured by Indians."

Major Rutherford nodded his head. "Good, Casselberry, good. I know how relieved you must be. Our scouting patrols must have missed her somehow. Give her my best wishes and tell her we hope she will feel well enough to come to our social next week."

"I'm sure she will, sir," Casselberry said. He nodded curtly at the two officers and stared at Spur for a long moment before he turned and walked away.

"Good man, that Casselberry," Major Rutherford said. "But he takes himself too seriously. You'd think he had to wade in and wipe out every Indian in all the Nations singlehanded. Glad you found his wife. She's a charmer and one of the smartest women on the post."

"It was pure chance that I ran into her, Major, pure chance," said Spur calmly.

Around midnight the party began breaking up.

Colonel Underhill withdrew early complaining of a bad cold. He wasn't missed. Spur was getting a definite feel for the command and some of the men who ran it. Major Rutherford seemed to hold the whole post together as the executive officer. Spur hadn't found a chance to talk to the major about the scout's problem. It was the kind of situation that could cause trouble for the whole post. Spur could see no immediate connection between the slaughter of the scout's family and the rifles, but he was keeping that option open. Buffalo Kane would be an ideal liaison between the army and the Indians. And the scout had an intense hatred for the officers on the post. He would think more about that.

Felicia Jones came by with her father, a balding captain with a paunch that showed he was a garrison soldier. Spur bet the man hadn't sat a horse in ten years. Felicia smiled.

"It was good to meet you, Colonel McCoy. We don't get many visitors here at Camp Sheridan, especially ones who can waltz so well. Will you be staying with us for long? The ladies are hoping that you will."

"I'm not rightly sure, Miss Jones. I hope so, just so I can have another dance with you."

She smiled over her shoulder at him as her father led her out the door.

Spur paid his respects to Mrs. Underhill, then walked out with Major Rutherford. They talked about the Black Hills Indian situation, then parted at the major's quarters. Spur was thinking more about the smile on Felicia's pretty face than he was about anything else, and consequently his guard was down. He came around the corner of the store and was heading for his bachelor quarters when a rifle fired fifty yards ahead of him and splinters exploded from the boards next to his head.

Spur dropped flat on the ground in half a second and crawled backwards to the protection of the sutler's building. The rifle boomed again and Spur felt the impact as the bullet smashed into the dirt beside him. He had just rounded the corner of the store when the third round slammed past.

Spur peered around the edge of the building. Who in the hell was shooting at him, and why?

# CHAPTER FOUR

Spur did not have his six-gun with him as he took another quick look around the corner of the sutler's store, then pulled back. He had no idea who had taken the shots at him. He listened. There was no outcry from the guards. Perhaps it was normal for rifle shots to punctuate the midnight calm at this army post, but he doubted it. A door slammed somewhere ahead and a light flickered on down the line of log houses. It was time to investigate.

Spur came around the corner in a crouch, running hard. He made it to the opposite building which was set twenty feet from the store. As quietly as possible, Spur edged to the far corner of the officers' quarters and looked around.

Nothing. The soft moonlight let him see plainly along the rear side of the row of attached quarters. No one was there in the fifty yard length of the line of buildings. He took two steps around the quarters and stopped. At his feet something glinted in the pale light. He bent down and found the brass casings of rifle bullets. He searched until he had found all three, then hurried back to his room. Spur struck a stinker and lit a lamp, then bolted the door and moved away from the window. He checked the shell casings and frowned. They were not standard army issue, he was sure of that. He would examine them in much more detail in the morning.

Suspects for the bushwhacking were hard to figure. The one possibility that immediately sprung to mind was Casselberry. The young lieutenant was obsessed with his army career, and Spur presented what could turn into a roadblock to that officer's future. It would take an extremely dedicated, even fanatical man to go to such lengths to forward his career.

Who else? The gun runner to the Indians was the second best suspect, whoever he was. But how would he know Spur's real mission so quickly? He had confided the true facts to no one. A leak of information from St. Louis or Washington D.C. was extremely unlikely. Perhaps the traitor was a thorough and cautious man, thinking a murdered colonel now would be better than the chance of exposure later.

Spur yawned. A real bed looked good to him. He enjoyed the nights on the trail but the ground was getting harder each time he slept out. He double checked the bolt on the front door, saw there was none on the back, and locked it with a simple skeleton-type key and wedged a wooden chair under the handle. If anyone tried to get in it would make a racket and alert him.

The secret agent stripped down to his underwear and slid into bed. The warm Nebraska weather

48

meant he would need only a sheet. He stretched out, thought for a moment about the day's events and knew that he had made a good start. The brass shell casings could be a big break for him. In two minutes he was sleeping.

Later, Spur had no idea how long it had been, he awakened, listened, and knew that the chair at the rear door was scraping as it moved. He was on his feet in a second, the big Merwin and Hurlburt .44 in his right hand as he moved silently on bare feet to the door. Spur waited until the door was pushed from the outside again, then flipped the chair away.

The person in the hall, fell forward into the room as the door swung inward. Spur dropped on top of the figure, pinning it to the floor. There was a shocked moment of total silence and no struggling at all.

"Oh, my goodness, hello," a softly familiar woman's voice said.

"Felicia?" Spur said, amazement showing in his voice. But he didn't move. Now he recognized the soft contours of a woman's body. "What are you doing breaking into my room?"

"Spur McCoy, I'll be glad to tell you. First, let me up, then put a blanket over your front window and light a lamp."

He grinned in the darkness. "Now that seems perfectly reasonable." Spur pulled a blanket from the bed, hung it over the small window that overlooked the parade grounds and then lit the lamp. He put on the chimney and turned up the wick, then looked at her. She wore a robe that brushed the floor and was buttoned tightly at her throat.

Spur felt no embarrassment standing there in his

underwear as she smiled at him.

"Well, Colonel McCoy, I see you were in bed after all. I had to stop by to tell you how much I enjoyed our dance tonight. But now I feel suddenly over-dressed."

She unbuttoned the robe and let it fall open. Felicia wore only a white, frilly chemise underneath, which stopped just below her crotch and on top revealed the delicious curving swell of both lovely breasts. Her legs were finely formed, slender, her waist narrowed delightfully, and now her face beamed with a combination of pride and desire. "I thought you might want to see what *I* wore to bed."

She let the robe slip to the floor and stood there waiting. A moment later she ran to him, her arms clasped around his back tightly as she pressed her body firmly against his.

Spur picked her up and carried her to his bed, lay her down gently, then leaned over and kissed her quivering lips. She pushed up to meet him and held the embrace as long as he did. When they parted she sighed and smiled.

"Oh, yes! I have been dreaming about how it would be to kiss you ever since we first met."

"And how was it?"

"Delicious! How about another?"

He kissed her again, and this time her lips parted. His tongue darted inside and she moaned in plea-sure. Then they began a brief skirmish of teasing tongues, and at last she gracefully conceded defeat. Already she was breathing faster. Spur left her for a moment, went to the back door and locked it again, then pushed the chair firmly under the handle.

"So we won't be disturbed," he said kissing her

nose, then finding her mouth again. As they kissed, one of her hands trailed down his shoulder to his thigh. Spur felt the most intense jolt of desire he had ever known exploding inside him, and he crushed her lips, as his hand moved to the fabric covering her breasts.

"Yes! Darling Spur, yes, touch me there! Oh, yes, fantastic, marvelous. Oh, just like that—don't stop —yes, I just love it!"

He caressed her breasts while she moaned in absolute pleasure, then gently lifted the short hem of the chemise, exposing her thick black thatch, tiny waist and full breasts.

She lifted her arms docilely and he pulled the chemise over her head, then looked down at her. She was perfectly formed, with generous hips and a slender waist. Spur raised her up to a sitting position and her breasts brushed against his chest.

"So beautiful!" Spur said. He bent and kissed each rosy nipple and as he did, she climaxed. Her whole body trembled and she held on to him, her nails sinking into his back as the ecstatic vibrations traveled through her frame, bringing from her small, intense cries of tormented pleasure and marvelously delicious quivering.

"Oh, my goodness!" she said softly. "I've never done that so quickly. You are the most marvelous lover in the whole world!"

"Sweetheart, we haven't even *started* yet!" Spur kissed her breasts again, nibbling on her nipples, turning them hard and pulsating and Felicia cried out sharply and climaxed again. She clung to him, then rolled over on the bed so she was on top of him. He felt her whole body vibrating in a series of delightful spasms. When at last she collapsed against him, resting her head on his chest, he asked, "Do you break into men's bedrooms often?"

"No—only once before, but I couldn't stand the thought of not being able to make love to you."

"When I played at your poker table and danced with you, I decided you were so shy I would have to make the first move if I were going to get to kiss you."

"That's exactly what I wanted you to think, because then those gossipy old biddies would think the same thing, and I'd be safe. You don't *know* what they can do. We're a closed society here. In a town, there is always the town drunk or the fallen woman to talk about. Here, all we have is each other. And the competition gets vicious. I'm so relieved that Janet Casselberry *wasn't* captured by the Indians. The old cats would have driven her out of her mind within a month, and her husband would no doubt have shot himself. It happened once that way in Texas where we were stationed."

One of her hands had been worming its way between their bodies as she spoke, and now it closed around Spur's erection. "Oh, my! Such a big boy, but I know what to do to bring him down a notch, to turn him into a long, soft worm." She rolled off and lay beside him, but kept her handhold and slowly stroked his manhood, then moved lower and gently massaged his scrotum and its heavy orbs.

"Oh, my goodness! I think we have a long, long night ahead of us. My guess is at least five times. What do you think, Spur?"

"At *least* five, I would think, pretty lady."

She bent over him then and began licking him, his

52

face, his ears, then down his neck to his chest where she licked and nibbled at his nipples.

"Just relax, big man. I won't hurt you. Felicia never has hurt any man she's made love to yet."

Spur lay there, relaxed and enjoying it. He marveled that this outwardly prim and proper girl could keep her intense sexuality so controlled and hidden on the small army post.

Her questing mouth moved lower and Spur felt her tongue tantalizing his long shaft. He started to stop her, then steeled himself and waited. Her tongue caressed his pulsating erection slowly, with a teasing perfection that soon left Spur gasping. Her lips toyed with the purpled head of his cock until Spur sputtered with frustration, then relaxed as he felt her hot mouth envelop it and her head began a steady bobbing up and down. His hips picked up the beat and worked against her. He lifted his head and was surprised to see how much of his shaft she had sucked into her mouth. He must be half way down her throat!

In spite of his session with Molly that afternoon, it didn't take Spur long to build up a wildly frantic head of steam. His hips bucked harder. He moaned and felt her hand slip around the base of his shaft so he wouldn't choke her.

To his surprise she began to hum a tune and it set him on fire. He moaned in pure animal lust, heard himself shout aloud as he erupted into the container of her mouth and then cry out again before he dropped flat on the bed, exhaustion smothering him like blankets, as Felicia licked him clean and then snuggled beside him.

"You were tremendous!" she said softly in his ear.

53

"Absolutely amazing! Let's make love every night you're in Camp Sheridan!"

He put his arm around her and hugged her naked body against his as he rested, still gasping for breath, hoping that he wouldn't die from the magnificient exertion of his climax.

As he recovered, they talked. He discovered she had been the housekeeper for her doctor father for the past four years, ever since her mother had died of the Texas fever. She told him that at first it had been fun; suddenly she was a woman with the duties of a housekeeper and even managing the household funds.

"But now I'm getting restless and tense. I want to get away from the army, to see San Francisco, and New York and Boston! Have you ever been to Boston?" She kept on talking without giving him a chance to answer. "I want to be rich. I won't settle for anything less. And someday I will be!"

As they both rested she toyed with the thick red hair on Spur's chest.

"I know I'll be rich because I like men, and I can please them. Why, right now I bet you'd do lots of things for me if I really wanted you to." She guided his hand to her breasts. "Now, Spur, honey baby, wouldn't you do good things for me?"

"Not for at least one hour," he said, then, changing the subject abruptly, "I had a little run-in with Lieutenant Casselberry earlier today. What do you know about him?"

"Not much. He's a spit and polish type, does everything by the book, all army. I swear he was born with those lieutenant's bars on! He'll probably be a general someday, but I still don't like him. I

54

guess you have to be something of a son-of-a-bitch to become a general." She giggled. "You jumped when I said those bad words, do you know that? I know worse ones. Want to hear me?"

"No," Spur said and reached his hand between her legs. She spread them at once and purred.

"*Now* you're going to do nice things for me, I just know that you are."

His hand slid up the inside of one thigh to the furry swatch, then down the other thigh and she tensed. When his fingers rubbed her mound, Felicia trembled.

"I don't know why it is, but I just *love* it when you touch me there. It's marvelous!"

His hand moved lower and his fingers expertly found her clitoris, rubbing with a gentle, insistent rhythm. She began crying softly. Tears trickled down her cheeks and her fingernails dug into his shoulders, then clawed down.

"Darling, I'm sorry," she gasped, patting his shoulder. Then she kissed him so hard his lips felt bruised, and all the time she continued to cry.

"I just can't help it. I feel so glorious, so beautiful that I could die. Have you ever felt that way?" She wiped tears from her eyes and moaned in gentle rapture. Her hips had started moving gently against his finger which found the hard node and played it like a mandolin.

Before he realized it she climaxed again. This time it was more physical. Her voice soared and wailed, then she jolted from side to side until he could hardly keep his finger in place and at last she jumped away from him and stood on the floor, pumping her hips at him in the air a dozen times, then fell back on the bed moaning softly.

"Now! Now you big cock, Spur. Now! I want you to shove it up into me so far I scream! Push it into me damnit, right now!"

She lay on her stomach on the bed and Spur went between her legs, lifted her hips, sliding past the brown rosebud of her anus to the pinkness of her slit. He probed carefully, then wedged in and a little at a time worked into her to his roots.

"Goodness, but that is fine!" she said. She crooned a small song as he settled in, then she looked over her shoulder at him.

"You just going to rest in there all night? Get something moving. How about a little action?"

Spur caught her under her hips and lifted her as he went to his knees, and holding her half in the air he pounded into her in a grinding, driving motion that kept Felicia moaning and yelping in the pleasure-pain of it. Spur knew it wouldn't take long. Rockets were going off and the red glare of their brilliance, the lightning-like streaks of passion slammed through him. He knew she was climaxing again as he did but he couldn't hear or see much of her reaction because of his own overpowering surges.

He let her down gently to the bed and lay on top of her, and she purred, "Yes, yes! Just crush me, I love it!" She laughed. "And this is what all those teachers and those old biddies who said they were my friends kept warning me against! 'Don't let a man have his way with you. Keep your skirts down. Never let a boy touch your breasts.' What a bunch of hypocrites! They were getting screwed every night and they didn't want me to know how good it was. I bet they were afraid I'd get their husbands interested." She was silent for a moment. "Hey, big Spur McCoy. What are you thinking about?"

"Right now?"

"Yes, right now."

"About you, how delicious you are. Wondering how long you can play around this way before you get pregnant. And wondering what you'll do if you get in the family way."

"Goodness gracious, don't even think about that! I'm having too much fun to worry. Anyway, I'll know quickly if I'm in the family way, and then I'll pick out the best man I can find and make him think he made me pregnant and I'll marry him. It just depends where I'm living then. If I'm in San Francisco it'll be harder—although I hear they are still short on women out there. I think I'll go next month."

She squirmed under him and he lifted away from her. She turned over at once.

"Hold me," she said.

"Yes." His arms went around her, and their bare torsos met, her breasts crushed against his chest.

"Good. I love being held this way. I guess . . . I guess I just love men!"

Spur laughed. "I'm damn glad of that!" He paused. "Shouldn't you be getting back?"

"No. When my father goes to sleep it takes a cannon shot to wake him. Anyway I live just two doors down." She wiggled in his arms, then settled down again. "I'm hungry." She pushed away from him, jumped off the bed and found her long robe on the floor. A moment later she had put it on and pulled the chair away from the door.

"I know you don't have any food in here. I'll slip back to our quarters and get some things. Don't go away, and *don't* get dressed. You promised me *six* times. You're going to have to prove it."

She was gone a moment later and Spur sat on the bed chuckling.

She was a delight, cute as a bouncing puppy, as sexy as a fancy lady and as unpredictable as a fresh-roped wild colt. She could also be a good source of information about the men in the officer corps, if he didn't push it too hard.

Before he had her evaluated completely, she was back. She carried a bottle of wine, a sack of crackers and a wedge of yellow cheese.

"Cheese and crackers in bed with some fairly good wine to wash it down."

He reached for the cork and began to loosen it. She produced two wine glasses and began slicing the cheese. He had a bite of the cheese and nodded. It was so sharp it seemed to slice his throat on the way down. Spur curved his hand around her naked side and captured one of her soft breasts. She pointed the knife at him.

"Still eager, I see. You give me another hour or two and I'm going to turn that cock of yours into a skinny little worm that won't have the strength to lift his head."

By four A.M. on Spur's Waterbury, the secret agent realized that Felicia had been right in her prediction.

"I told you!" she said and laughed. "Now it's time I get home. I'd better take all the evidence." She smiled. "You're good for a girl—but you already know that. Gentle, tender. Now, when can we get together again? This is Thursday. How about Saturday night? I'll invite you to our house for supper, then after you and father chat a while you can leave and I'll see you here after the doctor has his nightly nip and falls to sleep."

"Nothing I'd love better, Felicia, but I might not be on the post by then." He saw the pout forming on her mouth, and kissed it away.

"Tell you what. Let's call it a date, and if I can't come, I'll let you know early."

"You better come, Spur." She smiled and touched his limp penis. "I just *love* what that big lad down there does to me. You try. Please try, Spur."

He laughed gently, helped her into her robe and piled all of the remains of their midnight snack into her arms.

"I'll try," Spur said. No doubt about it, he would more than try.

# CHAPTER FIVE

Buffalo Kane had walked directly back to his quarters after talking to the new colonel. He was vaguely pleased. There was a feeling he couldn't quite pin down that this tall, strong individual was not the usual run of the army man. There was something about him that bred confidence.

Kane walked into his room, silently thanked the servant who had cleaned up his quarters the same as she had the officers', and flopped on the bed at the far side of the room. He found the half-full bottle of scotch whiskey near the front leg of the bed, picked it up, and stared at it a moment. Old John Barleycorn was his favorite companion these days. He hadn't done any work since his family was murdered, had done nothing but try to find out who had led that patrol. The enlisted men wouldn't even talk to him now, and the officers never had except on official business. They had told him he had to cut his hair and cut his beard. He'd told them all to go to hell. He had a scouting contract, and there wasn't a single word in it about how he wore his hair or his clothes. He tipped the bottle again, welcoming the raw whiskey as it sped down his throat and spread a warm glow throughout his body.

*Walking Fawn!* Kane blinked back hot tears as he thought of her. He'd been married to a white woman once, in Texas. He'd gone out on a scouting mission with the 5th Cavalry, and when he came back, his pretty young wife had left with a drummer who had been selling goods to the sutler's store. He never saw her again.

Kane blinked, wiped the wetness away from his eyes, and lifted the bottle.

He had found Walking Fawn after an army raid on an Indian village. She had seen her parents killed, her whole tribe nearly wiped out. Kane saw her escape into a patch of woods and waited until the company had left, then went in on foot and found her huddled against a tree, sobbing. She had been only sixteen years old, but he had used the few words he knew of Cheyenne and convinced her he meant her no harm. She went with him and they set up a crude camp half a day's ride from his post. Those had been the good times. Walking Fawn had been a proud Cheyenne, and made him remember it, but she was also eager to learn. He taught her English and she had picked it up quickly, eagerly. Their first son was born a year later, a healthy boy Buffalo had promptly named Karl after his father.

Buffalo would never forget the first time the men and officers on the post in Kansas learned that he had an Indian wife living off the post. The officers had selected the biggest, meanest enlisted man in camp to call Kane out. Kane remembered it as if it were yesterday.

"Hey, squaw man!" Corporal Larson bellowed. "Get your sneaky ass out here. I'm gonna shove your asshole right out your mouth 'fore I'm done with you."

Kane had been in the sutler's store getting some chewing tobacco, and had been hurried outside by the merchant, who didn't want the upcoming fight to take place on his premises.

Buffalo stepped into the blazing Kansas sun blinking, and Larson attacked him from the shadows. Larson was over six feet, as wide as a pair of plow handles, and loved to fight dirty. He caught the still-squinting Buffalo and drove him backwards into the street, ramming him into the dirt and slamming on top of him with his 230 pounds of muscle. With a quickness that surprised the big man, Buffalo squirted out of his arms and leaped to his feet. He kicked his assailant in the ribs and again in the shoulder before Larson could get up.

"Gonn' kill your ass!" Larson roared. He came off the ground in a charging crouch and swung a massive fist at Buffalo. But the target wasn't there when the fist sailed through the air. Instead, Kane slammed down his own fist as hard as he could against Larson's wrist. The force of the blow snapped the wrist bone with a sound that could be heard halfway across the parade ground.

Larson screeched in pain. Anger and fear, mixed with a new respect for the squaw man, filled his eyes, then he unleashed a string of profanity ending with a scream for someone to go get the doctor.

"Lucky son-of-a-bitch!" Larson screamed at

Kane. "Wait until the wrist gets healed. I'll kill you with my bare hands!"

Buffalo Kane laughed at the corporal where he sat in the dust.

"Like hell you will, Larson. You'll never fight as well again. You'll always be afraid somebody else might get 'lucky' like I did. And you'll never lay a hand on me again, Larson, 'cause if you do, I'll cut your balls off!" Buffalo Kane turned and walked to the stables, took a horse and went home to his family. Nobody, enlisted man nor officer, bothered him about his Indian family after that.

Kane shivered, just remembering Kansas. But this was Nebraska, it was a different post, and his family was dead. He lifted the bottle and drained the last of the whiskey. Two hours of steady drinking and the booze hadn't affected him. Goddamnit, he couldn't even get drunk!

Kane remembered that first summer with Walking Fawn. She was such a little thing, barely four feet ten inches tall, and as slender as a willow shoot. He had never known any person as alert, as sensitive to nature as she had been.

Once they were walking through a patch of hardwood trees. She stopped and motioned for him to wait. She stayed quiet for a minute, then pointed ahead and to the left. A doe with a spotted fawn walked into view, the mother grazing, the youngster prancing around her. The pair nibbled on some leaves, and the fawn tried to nurse but the doe brushed him away and they moved on into the deeper woods.

Walking Fawn turned and smiled radiantly at

Kane. He reached down, picked her up and hugged her. She frowned and pretended that she didn't like it, but at last she put her arms around his neck and softly kissed his cheek.

In most of their camps near the various army posts she could find most of their food from the land. She snared rabbits, dug roots and picked berries, and if there were fish, she knew how to catch them in small reed or willow mesh traps.

Little by little she had taught Buffalo how to live with nature, to accept both the bounty and the harsh laws of the natural world, instead of trying to bludgeon the land into subservience to the needs of man.

It was Walking Frawn who named him Buffalo. She later told him that first day that she thought he was a man-buffalo come to rescue her from the pony soldiers. From then on he discarded his given name and used Buffalo.

This small, tough, Indian girl, had given him so much. She had brought to his life form, design and purpose. He was looking forward to the time when he could find a small plot of arable ground and settle down to being a kind of a farmer—maybe raise a few head of cattle, sell some, grow their own food. He would raise his two boys to know better than he had.

That was his dream, but it had been shattered that afternoon more than a month before by the fusillade from six Spencer repeating carbines. There weren't a lot of Spencers in the army, but a few dozen 1860 Spencers were around.

He knew the weapon well. It was a .52 caliber using number 56 Spencer rim-fire cartridges and had a twenty-two inch round barrel with three rifled grooves. Its total length was thirty-nine inches and it weighed a little over eight pounds, had blade front sight and sliding leaf rear sight. All the metal was blued except the receiver which was case-hardened in mottled colors.

Kane could imagine the troopers that fatal day with their Spencers. The picture came to him once more of his two sons playing outside the hut near the big cottonwood tree. The rifles fired again and again, cutting down the two children, then the big bullets ripping into Walking Fawn's soft flesh as she screamed and raced outside to help her sons.

He saw the rifles firing and firing.

And Buffalo's family died.

In less than three minutes they were all dead. Then the troopers had left, quickly. One set of hoof-prints showed that one rider had moved around the bodies. At least they had not been further violated.

Buffalo Kane stared at the empty bottle, then threw it across the room where it broke against the rough wall and fell into pieces to the floor.

Somebody was going to pay.

Somebody was going to admit to the crime, and then Buffalo Kane was going to shoot that bastard six times, make him suffer as much as possible, damn well make him know *why* he was dying.

Damn sure!

Drunk, Goddamn finally got drunk. Buffalo tried to get his clothes off. Had a bed, didn't have to sleep like a trail drive cowhand . . . Take off his clothes . . . At least his boots. Man slept better . . . slept better with his . . .

A moment later Buffalo Kane's head fell to one side, his mouth sagged open and he snored.

Kane dreamed as he did every night. This time he arrived just in time. He set up the Gatling gun and wiped out the patrol before the men could get off the first shot. He saved the lieutenant, and marched him up to the commanding general's office in Omaha and made him confess that he had tried to kill Kane's family. The general had ripped the indicators of rank from the officer's uniform and spit on him. Then ceremoniously, the general had taken out his pearl-handled .44 and shot the faceless officer in the head.

Kane moaned as he rolled in the bed, but no matter how he tried, he still couldn't see the face of the dead officer. Who was he? Who was the murderer who had killed Buffalo Kane's family?

# CHAPTER SIX

The morning after his marathon with Felicia Jones, Spur woke with a groan and sat up slowly. She had drained him within a pair of deep breaths of all his energy. But it had been worth it. What a feisty, sexy little fireball! It was five-thirty, and he shaved and trimmed his moustache. He washed the sleep from his face and did two dozen quick pushups, then a hundred jumping jacks and washed down his face, head and bare torso.

That morning he put on a regulation dark blue army shirt, and lighter blue pants. Then he pulled on slightly worn army boots and a tan, wide-brimmed low-crowned army campaign hat. To complete the effect he tied a yellow kerchief around his throat, buckled on an issue cartridge belt and slid his big .44 into the holster. It was the only uniform he had with him. His full colonel's eagles gleamed in silver on his shoulder epaulets.

He had breakfast with the officers, dining well on eggs fresh from the sutler's chickens, hashbrowns and onions and half a dozen large hotcakes and syrup. He talked with several of the officers he had met, then went directly to the camp commander's office.

Colonel Underhill had recovered from his malaise of last night and sat behind his desk, his thin face puzzled over some problem sketched in front of him on a pad of paper. He noticed Spur come in, glanced up and saw the twin eagles, and eased to his feet.

"Good morning, Colonel McCoy."

"Good morning, Colonel. I need to have a short conference with you this morning. Last night someone tried to kill me."

Colonel Underhill's head snapped up and he stared Spur in the eye. "Then it's true. You aren't here on some survey. I've heard the junior officers say you're a spy for Phil Sheridan."

"General Sheridan doesn't even know I'm here, Colonel. My orders come from much higher up than that." Spur sat down in the chair across the desk, and the camp commander waited until he was settled, then sat himself.

"Colonel Underhill, I must insist that what I'm about to tell you must remain in the strictest of confidence."

"Naturally, sir. I understand."

"Your casualty figures for the past three months are interesting, Colonel. You show thirteen troopers killed and forty-seven wounded. But the important part is that all these casualties but one were caused by rifle fire. As I'm sure you know, most of the army's casualties from Indians are caused by arrows. Most of our fights are against bows and arrows, not against rifles. Do you know how this happened to several of your patrols in your section?"

"No, sir. It's been worrying me."

"The problem is getting worse. Indians in this sector are somehow acquiring large numbers of rifles and ammunition. My job, Colonel Underhill, is to find the supply route, snuff it out and locate whoever is supplying the weapons."

"I've heard of civilians trading guns to the Indians for all sorts of goods—even gold."

"That isn't the case here, Colonel. There are no civilians in this area who could barter with the Sioux. My instructions are to take a careful look at some far west army establishments in this sector and determine if any of the rifles falling into Indian hands are coming directly or indirectly from army supplies."

Colonel Underhill leaped to his feet. "Sir!" he thundered. "That's an insult! Are you accusing me or any of my men of trading with the enemy? Accusing me of *treason?*" Underhill's face had flushed. He was breathing so heavily he almost panted. His eyes were wild, furious, darting glances at Spur, then around the room.

Spur crossed his legs and leaned back in the chair.

"Sit down, Colonel. I'm not accusing you or your men of anything. What I am saying is that it is highly probable that the savages have somehow obtained army rifles and ammunition from this post or some other, and it is my job to find out what supply route is used and to stop it."

"*Goddamn you!* You are implying that me or my men are selling rifles to the enemy! In my own office you're accusing me of treason! I don't have to stand for that!" He marched around the room, his arms

69

flailing the air, his face dark red now, his eyes wary, one hand near the sabre that hung on his belt. He picked up a chair from the far side of the room and threw it at the wall. A leg broke off the chair and it crashed to the floor.

"I don't have to put up with this! I'll send word to Phil today that you're a disgrace to the uniform. I don't care what your higher authority says. I've served my country for almost thirty years!"

He stormed to the door and opened it, looked out onto the parade grounds. For a moment the colonel shivered, pulling himself together, then he staightened his shoulders and closed the door gently. When he turned around his complexion had returned to normal, his eyes were placid and his breathing was even, quiet.

"Now, Colonel McCoy, you say you're here to investigate those stolen army rifles. Good thinking. We have lost a few recently. Not a lot—one or two here, one there. A rifle missing from the stack in the barracks. Supply reports another gone from the armory. Nothing you can trace or pin down. Good thinking. Perhaps there *has* been some kind of a traitor right here at Camp Sheridan. You probably will want to consider Camp Robinson, Fort Fetterman and Camp Brown as well."

Spur nodded, completely astonished. The colonel had exploded before Spur's eyes into a raging maniac, then within a few seconds had reverted to a logical, reasonable individual. There was something definitely wrong here.

"Fine, Colonel. I wanted you to know exactly why I am here. As far as the men are concerned, I am still conducting a survey for the Quartermaster Corps.

This is something they can understand, and we won't scare off anyone who might have some connection with a larger conspiracy, if there is one. And if we're successful, Colonel, we should be able to reduce your casualty figures a great deal. At least we can cut off the supply source of the ammunition. Rifles are relatively benign without cartridges."

Colonel Underhill chuckled. "Quite right, Colonel, absolutely right. Oh, could I ask your authorization again for this job."

Spur smiled. "As I told you, the commanding general of the Quartermaster Corps."

Colonel Underhill nodded. "I understand. Some things I get to know, and some I don't. Anything I can do for you, just let me know."

Underhill's uniform hung on him like it was draped over a picket fence. His smile was more sincere now but looked out of place on his large head that slanted slightly forward.

Spur McCoy went out the door into the harsh Nebraska sunshine and a wind that sent grit stinging against his cheeks.

Next stop on Spur's agenda was the supply room, the supply sergeant. There must be one—or whatever he was called now. Spur had been away from the army for several years and knew some things had changed.

The supply and equipment storage area was at the center of the five administrative buildings. It was one story and made of bricks. Just inside the door sat a barrel-chested corporal, clean shaven and totally bald. Bushy eyebrows shaded small eyes that looked reasonably intelligent. He snapped to attention and saluted.

"Colonel, sir. Corporal Kramer."

Spur returned to salute and the corporal stood stiffly at attention.

"At ease, Corporal Kramer. You probably know why I'm here—the survey." Spur looked at him closely. Kramer was an old time soldier who had found light duty. He had learned the army system and benefited from it, and had mastered the art of army politics. It was a wonder he was only a corporal.

Spur dug into his pocket and took out the three shell casings he had picked up the previous night.

"A small problem for you, Corporal. A friend gave me these shell casings and wants me to find some ammunition for him. He says it's army issue, only most posts don't have any. Can you help me? He didn't even tell me what kind of a weapon takes these rounds."

Corporal Kramer took the brass casings and scowled at them a moment. "Sir, I think you're in luck. You're right, that ain't one of our usual rounds. Looks like what we used to use in the old 1860 Henry repeating rifle. Near ten thousand of them were made. Lots were lost during the War when the Yankees used them." He turned over the cartridge and looked at the base.

"Yep, look here, Colonel. See that 'H' stamped on there? That's for B. Tyler Henry who invented that weapon. The Rebs used to say the Henry was the damned Yankee rifle that a body could load on Sunday and fire all week. Had a tubular magazine under the barrel that held twelve rounds. It's a .44 caliber, of course. You want me to see if we'uns got any rounds? Must be two or three Henrys still in camp."

"Yes, Corporal. If you don't have any, I'd like the names of the men who have the weapons. Perhaps I could persuade them to sell me a few cartridges."

"No problem, Colonel. Give me an hour or so to check and I'll have some rounds for you and the names."

"Thank you, Corporal. Now, about this survey. How many spare rifles and carbines do you keep in stock?"

"Spares? Damn, sir, don't know right off. Got some in I haven't checked out yet. Boxes. Then we have three or four that need some repair work." He paused. "I can get you the figures, sir, but that's going to take a little longer."

"No rush, Corporal. By noon will be fine. I'll also want a list of all rifles and carbines by serial number and which man they have been assigned to."

The corporal raised his eyebrows. "That's going to take some doing, sir, but I'll try to have it by this afternoon."

"Fine, Corporal. Have the lists delivered to me at my quarters." Spur turned and left, pondering what the corporal had told him. Three Henry repeating rifles in camp, and one of them had been used in his bushwhacking. That should make them easy to find.

Spur heard a volley of shots and moved quickly to a vantage point. He found a company of men firing at a stationary target. Each trooper was given twenty rounds and was scored on his efforts at the large bull's-eye target 50 yards away. Spur watched for a while and kept his eye open for a Henry repeater but didn't see any.

He checked his Waterbury and found he had time to make a walking tour of camp before checking back with Corporal Kramer. When at last he returned to the armory, the corporal had some answers for him. There were thirty-four spare carbines and rifles in operating condition and twelve that needed repair.

"But there are five missing, sir," Kramer said in a rush. "I don't know for the life of me where they got to. They ain't signed out to anyone, and they ain't here!"

"Put that in your report to me, soldier. I want the type weapons and the serial numbers. Right now!"

"Yes, sir! I swear I don't know what happened. Nobody checks out rifles and carbines except me. No chance they could just be lost. Some son-of-a-bitch *stole* them from me! I'm gonna have somebody's hide."

"So am I, Corporal. So am I. Now show me where you keep the weapons."

The enlisted man led Spur into the storeroom, down an aisle and to the back wall where the rifle rack held the weapons. They had a chain through the trigger guards and were padlocked on each end. One of the rifles was four feet long. Spur looked at it and pointed.

"Is that one of your Henry repeating rifles?"

"Yes, sir. Here are the names of the troopers who have the other two. Some of the platoon leaders like to have one long gun along for longer range sharpshooting."

Spur took the piece of paper and put it in his pocket. "Finish that report with the serial numbers and get it to my quarters, Corporal." He turned and walked out of the supply room.

It was time for Spur to go to the commander's

quarters for the noon meal. Grace Underhill had invited him during the dance the preceding evening. As he walked, he thought about the camp commander again. The man certainly had a variety of personalities. He had been cold, irritated, angry when Spur first arrived, then had turned into a raging maniac when Spur suggested the rifles the Indians were using were army issue. But seconds later he had changed again into a relatively normal man, eager to please a superior officer, and to get at the root of the problem. Underhill could develop into a definite threat to Spur's mission.

Spur returned a few salutes and then walked into the commander's office. A sergeant at the side desk braced at attention and reported that Col. McCoy could go into the living quarters. The sergeant knocked, then opened the door for Spur.

Grace Underhill met him with a firm handshake. She wore what he guessed was her best dress, light blue and covered with bows and ruffles.

"Colonel, you don't know how exciting it is having you here!" she bubbled. "We get so few visitors that we must make a fuss over them. Ezekiel is polishing his boots—he'll be right here. I told him he had to be on his best behavior."

Someone came through a door behind them and Spur turned. He caught his breath and he knew his eyes widened. Her skin was a light dusky tan shade and her dark hair was braided on each side and hung to her waist. She was obviously and proudly Indian, but Spur had no idea of what tribe. She was dressed neatly and attractively in rose-colored flowered calico. Her face was round, her features softly etched, with almond shaped eyes, a small, pert nose, parted lips that glistened as if she had just licked them, and a strong chin that now lifted a little as her glance found his and locked on it.

Mrs. Underhill turned. "Yes, Chitsa, I'm glad you decided to come have dinner with us. I *told* you Colonel McCoy is not like most of the officers. I sensed that right away. Colonel McCoy, this is my ward, Chitsa. She is like my own daughter since I never had any children of my own. She has been with us now for almost fifteen years. Chitsa, this is Colonel Spur McCoy."

The girl took in a quick breath and bowed her head an inch, then straightened and looked up. She was tiny, under five feet tall, Spur guessed, with the slender but voluptuous body of a woman. He decided she must be nearly twenty years old.

"I understand, Colonel McCoy, that you do not favor slaughtering every Indian you see just because she has red skin."

Spur laughed and saw that she was not offended. "You are quite correct. But just as there are vicious, unprincipled cowardly, and rebellious white men and women, I assume the same is true of the Negro, the German, the Japanese, the Eskimo and the Indian. It is only those whom I would find objectionable."

"You see, Chitsa? I told you he was cultured and sophisticated, and could keep up with your book learning. Gracious, this poor girl has had nobody but me to talk to for so long, but she reads so many books. We tote around more books than you could shake a dead rattlesnake at, and she reads most of the day."

"Now, Grace, that's not entirely true. At the last

76

camp, I used to play our neighbor's piano."

"Yes, dear, and I wish we had one for you here. When we go back to Washington, we'll be sure to get one. Oh, here is Ezekiel now. Let's go in to dinner."

Colonel Underhill was in his work blues, the same uniform that Spur wore. They moved into a dining room Spur had not seen the previous night. To his surprise it was rather luxurious. A thick carpet covered the floor and the single window was draped with heavy curtains which let in the light but kept out most of the heat. Framed pictures adorned the papered walls and a cherrywood dining table set for four stood in the center. Matching cherrywood chairs had artfully stitched needle work seats.

Grace indicated where each should sit. Spur quickly took Chitsa's chair and held it for her, then sat at her right between the ladies.

"I trust the colonel has had a productive morning?" Underhill began.

"Hush, Ezekiel!" Grace cut in quickly. "We are not going to talk army. We get quite enough of that. I was hoping that Colonel McCoy could tell us something of what's happening in Washington. Is General Grant really going to double the size of the army? You know, Ezekiel was a brevet major general during the War. My, those were the days! We were in Washington for most of the War, did he tell you that? We miss the good things civilization can provide. Out here, we feel, cut off, stranded."

"Mrs. Underhill, I doubt very much that President Grant will be able to expand the army. We're at peace, and most of our citizens have bad memories of the Civil War. And remember, President Grant is just getting started. He has a lot to learn about Washington politics. It will take him at least a year to get many of his programs underway."

They went on talking for an hour as they ate roast pheasant with crabapple jelly, assorted vegetables, and tarts. It seemed like an unusual lunch, but Spur decided that was the way Mrs. Underhill had planned it.

Several times Spur noticed Chitsa watching him, a shy smile on her softly pretty face. She did a lot of the talking, and Colonel Underhill was plainly disturbed by her vivacity.

When the women were about to retire, Chitsa came up to him and paused a moment, then smiled. "I want to remember one army officer who does not hate all Indians on sight," she said. Then she smiled. "You actually think of us as human beings, which is a great step forward." She laughed. "I bet your general doesn't know about this!" She took his hand and shook it solemnly. "Thank you again." Then she turned and left. Spur felt a strange tingle of excitement when she touched him, and now as he watched her leave, her shoulders squared, her head held high, he was determined to see her again as soon as circumstances permitted.

# CHAPTER SEVEN

Lt. Casselberry took his noon meal in his quarters. The officers' mess had butchered a steer from the camp herd last night and everyone had steak or ground meat. He cut into his steak, saw the rich, red blood seep out and smiled, then put a large bite into his mouth.

"I hope it's cooked right, Neil. I did it just the way you said."

Janet Casselberry had combed her hair carefully and tied it with a ribbon so it fell down her back in a golden stream. She had scrubbed her face until it glowed and put just a touch of rouge on her lips. She was wearing a checked gingham dress that was just a little tight and showed off her breasts and small waist. She sat across from him, nibbling at her steak.

"Yes, Jan, yes it's good. It's been a long time since I've had steak. Damn good!"

"Neil, after you eat, could we have time for a talk?

I've been so miserable these past two days. We have to get this straightened out."

"There is nothing to discuss," Neil said, his voice turning cold. "We simply watch the reaction of the men and more importantly, of the officers' wives. After you pass that test, we'll talk. If they figure out what actually happened, I will ask for a transfer as quickly as possible. Then we'll discuss our future."

"Neil, I need you! I've never asked you this before . . . but would you, right now, come into the bedroom, and make me feel needed and whole again?"

"*What?* It's not your place to suggest . . . I'm shocked, Janet."

She stood and moved behind him, bent and put her arms around him. "Neil, for God's sake, I need you to make love to me!"

He turned and saw that she had unbuttoned her bodice. Both full, pink-tipped breasts swung gently in front of his face.

"Oh, damn!" He stood and had to stop himself from caressing her breasts. "Janet, I'm as confused as you are. I don't know for sure if those Indians raped you or not. You might have been sleeping, or unconscious, or . . ."

"I told you, they were afraid once they saw the camp—they were rushing away. They never did a thing but make me take my blouse and chemise off."

"Oh, God how I wish I could believe that!" His hand curved around one of her breasts, then he groaned and pulled away. He ran for the front door, grabbing his hat and sabre as he went, tears stinging his eyes. Just outside the door he stopped, turned and went back inside.

"Janet, I'm sorry. I just can't . . . can't trust myself to love you, not yet. *I must be sure.* I know—I have your word, but a man must sometimes have more than that. We must be sure of the people here, then I'll know for sure."

He ran to her, caressed and kissed her naked breasts, then stood and wiped tears from his eyes. "In another week or two we should know. It won't be very long. Try to understand what this is doing to *me.* You were half of my life, half of my dreams, and now this ugly . . . those savages . . . It's just almost more than I can bear!" He wiped his eyes again, straightened his sabre and walked out the door, closing it gently.

Janet locked the door and ran sobbing into her bedroom. For a moment she touched her breasts, remembering his caress, the touch of his lips. The tears came then, floods of them. She wanted him so much! She needed him to make her feel like a woman again! Her hand rubbed her nipples. It felt so good! It wasn't his hand, but it was a caress. She thought back, remembering their wedding night, and slowly she began to smile. Her hand rubbed harder now, and her other hand pulled up her long skirt and deftly wormed inside her cotton drawers. This is wrong! she told herself. But I need it so badly, she answered, and her hand explored downward until it found her soft nest, already damp with desire. Janet touched it and her body quivered as she moaned softly and pretended that it was her wedding night . . .

After his noon meal, Spur made the rounds of the

barracks, the mess, the stables, justifying his protective cover of making a survey. He had a pad of paper on which he jotted down notes, and at times even looked interested. He ate supper at the officers' mess and then checked over the list of names, weapons and the records of the two enlisted men who had the Henry repeating rifles. Nothing seemed to make sense from the list, or the group of missing rifles. Wearily he decided to get to bed early and perhaps make up for some of the sleep he had missed the night before.

As Spur lowered the light in his desk lamp, a solitary rider galloped out the far gate and rode toward the river. The horse was an army mount, and an army man sat there, riding easily. There was no hesitation. The rider knew exactly where he was going and how to get there.

He rode with skill, and from time to time the moonlight glinted off gold bars on his shoulders. The rider was an officer. Ten minutes away from the camp, he came to a ford over the White River and crossed, letting the horse walk. On the far side, the officer turned and rode upstream, away from the camp and deeper into Indian territory.

A mile upstream he stopped, checking the tie-downs on a long blanket-covered package behind his saddle. When he was satisfied with the lashings, he crooked one leg on the saddle and built himself a cigarette. The tobacco filled the trough in the white cigarette paper and he put the sack of makings in his pocket, then rolled the paper between his fingers so it formed a thin tube. He expertly licked the flap and sealed it, then looked at it in the faint light. A little lumpy, but it would have to do. A stinker flared and he lit it, put his foot back in the stirrup and rode upstream again, heading in a southwesterly direction.

After another half hour of slow riding along the river bank, he came to a lightning-struck cottonwood that was now little more than a jagged, two-forked snag towering over a bend in the White. He got off his mount, tied her to a small tree and pulled down the blanket-wrapped package.

The officer sat against the base of the tree, rolled another cigarette and lit it openly, then smoked as he listened to the night sounds of the prairie. It was all totally foreign to him, but he would make it work *for* him, not against him. He would turn *everything* into an advantage for himself.

He sat there for fifteen minutes, and then had a feeling that someone else was nearby. A few seconds later the feeling became a certainty when an arrow whispered through the air and thunked into the dead cottonwood tree two feet over his head.

The army officer didn't move. He smiled, knowing that his contact was coming, and that the final negotiations would go forward as planned.

After another five minutes he heard a horse and soon an Indian pony came into view over the slight rise. An Indian wearing a beaded headband, loin cloth and moccasins rode the pony. The Indian carried something as he slid off the pony. He tied the animal to a bush, then walked up and squatted a few feet from the officer.

"You bring?" the Indian asked.

"Damn right. Did *you* bring?"

The Indian held out a rawhide sack closed at the top with a drawstring. It was eight inches long and heavy.

The officer pulled his bundle forward, untied the leather thongs from it and rolled out two army rifles and a carbine. In a small square box were two hundred cartridges.

The Indian nodded and handed the heavy rawhide bag to the officer who undid the rawhide and laces and looked inside. He poured some of the chunks into his hands, then struck a stinker match to check.

He grunted, evidently satisfied.

"Yeah, some of it looks right. But remember, just the squaw clay. That's all we want. Not the other rocks. Understand that? Just squaw clay."

The Indian nodded. "Bang, bang?" he said, indicating the weapons.

The next ten minutes were spent showing the brave exactly how the cartridges went into the rifles, and how they were fired. When he was through with the instruction, the officer removed the ammunition and had the Indian load each weapon, then fire and reload. With each round the brave became more excited.

"Many, many!" the brave said when he had the package wrapped up again and ready to travel.

"Fifty, you understand. Fifty."

The Indian shook his head. The officer held up both his hands with fingers extended. "Ten," he said. He then closed his fists and opened them again saying "twenty," and worked up to fifty. At last the brave understood.

"For fifty rifles, you must bring me two powder kegs filled with squaw clay. The kegs will be at this spot tomorrow night. You come pick them up."

It took another ten minutes to get the arrangements straight for the sale. At last the Indian nodded, clutched the rifles and leaped on his pony. He galloped off into the night without a backward glance.

"Uppity son-of-a-bitch!" the army man said, then hefted his sack, tucked it inside his shirt and rode for the camp.

As he approached Camp Sheridan, the officer slid off his mount and watched. He gave a poor imitation of a night hawk's cry, but there was no answering call. A half hour later the officer tried the call again, and this time the guard near the rear entrance to the camp responded with the same call. The officer mounted, rode through the gate and quickly put his horse in a stall at the back of the stable.

The guard who let the officer in watched the man ride inside. He didn't have the slightest idea what the lieutenant was doing out there in the dark, but that was his affair. The trooper would get a two-dollar gold piece tomorrow—that was all he was interested in, and all he needed to know. The less he knew, the less anyone could make him tell.

# CHAPTER EIGHT

Spur McCoy kept no notes on current assignments, but he did keep a kind of report diary. He noted each day where he was and generally what he was doing. He had just finished a two-line report on the day and put the pad and pencil away when a knock sounded on his door. He went to the front and opened it, but saw no one. He closed it and bolted it, then heard the knock again.

This time he went to the rear door and opened it. He fully expected to see Felicia Jones. Instead, he found a tentative and slightly embarrassed Janet Casselberry. She looked both ways along the darkened buildings.

"Colonel, could I talk to you a moment?"

"Yes, of course, come in." Spur opened the door and she entered quickly.

"Thank you. I didn't want anyone to see me come in. You know—it would look bad, somebody might talk."

He nodded. She wore a simple dress in some cotton fabric that fit snugly around her breasts and covered her from neck to floor.

"I . . . I just wanted to thank you again." She looked up, her pretty eyes pleading with him. She blinked the tears from her eyes. "Oh, Colonel, I simply don't know what to do! My husband is still so hostile about everything." She covered her face with her hands. "Sorry—I'm doing this very badly. I should never have come this way." She tried to dry her tears with her sleeve. Then she squared her shoulders and faced Spur. "Colonel, I'm a woman of my word. I told you I would thank you more appropriately later. Now I want to do that. But I . . . I have nothing of value to offer you . . ." She stopped and started for the door. "I'm simply no good at this!" Suddenly she stamped her foot, turned and marched back to him, standing so close that her breasts touched his chest. She looked up defiantly. "Colonel, the only thing I can offer is myself—to express my gratitude." She put her arms around his back and pressed hard against him, resting her cheek on his shoulder. "Neil even sleeps on the couch, he won't touch me. If you would help *me,* Colonel, I would be ever so grateful." She pulled his head down so she could kiss his lips and he felt her tongue against his mouth.

"Colonel, I've only made love to one man in my whole life, but now I *need* someone. I'm willing to . . ."

"Janet, I talked with your husband. I know how he feels. You don't have to do this. In a week or two it will be all settled down and he'll be loving you again—in every way."

"I tried to tell myself that. But this noon I tried to

seduce him. I couldn't. It made me think. . . . made me think I'm old, and homely and ugly and no man will have me. I know it's not logical, that it's silly—still . . ."

She looked up at him and he bent and kissed her lips. This time his were open as well. Her tongue darted into his mouth and she gave a little sigh. When the long kiss ended she moved her hands to her throat and unfastened one button. Then she looked up shyly.

"Would you . . . do you want to help me take this off?"

"Janet, you mustn't do this. You are a beautiful young lady. You're so pretty, with all that long blonde hair and those big brown eyes, that any man on the post would give a month's pay to help you undress just to look at you. You have a marvelous figure, your breasts are fantastic, your waist is so small and your hips . . . Are you sure you don't want to wait out that two weeks?" Spur wondered if he could wait another two minutes.

In response, she caught one of his hands and held it over one of her full breasts.

"Spur, please love me," she whispered.

His hands worked as if of their own volition, as he caressed her.

"Spur, you don't know how fine that feels! Just to know that a man is a little bit interested . . ."

"Janet, never, never question your appeal to the opposite sex again. Shall I show you exactly *how* interested I am?" He took one of her hands and pushed it down between their bodies to his fly where a large bulge had developed.

"Oh, thank God," she said. She left her hand there, rubbing him tenderly.

He opened the rest of the buttons on her bodice and at once it was apparent she wore nothing underneath. Her soft breasts were unconfined and his hands devoured them. Her nipples surged upward, pink and hot in their surrounding seas of softer pink areolas. He bent and kissed each nipple and Janet shivered.

"Nice, so nice!" When his head came up she kissed his lips.

Spur picked her up and carried her to the army bed and put her down gently. He kissed both her breasts, then her open mouth, and she sighed contentedly.

"Hey, I thought *you* were going to seduce *me*," he said jokingly.

She smiled ruefully. "I don't have much experience."

"Try—I'll cooperate," Spur assured her.

She smiled in that soft, enigmatic way, and slid off the bed. Quickly she lifted off her dress, then pushed down two petticoats and a pair of white drawers and stood before him beautifully naked.

"Marvelous!" Spur said. "Now get to work." He sat on the bed and played with her breasts as she started undressing him. At last he helped her, sucking one of her nipples as he did so. She made a little noise in her throat as she pulled down his trousers and then the short underwear.

"Oh!" she gasped as she saw his erection. "I've never seen anything so huge! Can I touch it?"

"You better!"

She caught his penis in her hand, marveling at its size and heat.

"I think it might *burn* me!" she said, excitement in her words. Then she pushed Spur flat on his back and straddled him, sitting on his belly and leaning forward so one breast dangled over his lips. Spur chuckled, caught it in his mouth and sucked. As he did, he felt her climaxing. It was short and sharp, a double jolt that contorted her face and brought a series of small sharp yelps. Then it was done and she smiled tremulously.

She let him suck on both breasts, then moved forward until her fuzzy swatch was close to his face.

"Eat me!" she said with surprising command in her voice.

Spur lifted his head as she moved forward and pushed his face into her crotch, his tongue reaching for her heartland, touching it, digging into the soft petals and plunging inside.

Janet gave a piercing wail and fell back on the bed, her whole body quivering in a gigantic climax. The wail turned into moans of delight until the last of the tremors stopped and she tapered off into a soft, cooing rest.

At last she lay on her stomach, propped her chin under her hands and stared at him. "I didn't think a man would really *do* that. It was incredible. Can I travel with you and be your pet?" she teased, then crawled over him and kissed his throbbing manhood. "Since I'm seducing you, I want to be on top. I've never been on top before."

Spur lay on his back, spread his legs and laced his fingers together behind his head. "I'm all yours, Janet. Do with me what you will."

She giggled, went to her hands and knees and bent taking his cock in her mouth and licking it tenderly.

Then she hovered over him on her knees, positioned herself again and then leaned forward and lowered herself onto his shaft. Spur felt a surge of emotion as he slowly slid into her. She was panting, and then she groaned as he felt himself drive into her. She leaned forward, her knees still bent, and kissed his lips.

She began rocking back and forth, riding him like a spring stallion, making more little moves and creating delicious friction unlike anything Spur had ever experienced.

"Wonderful!" she moaned once, then he saw her eyes glaze and her breath come in a surging gasp as she began trembling violently. She fell on top of him, shattered by the ecstasy within her.

She pushed up from him and he saw sweat beading her forehead. "Oh, Spur, it's never, never, *never* been so marvelous! Good, but never like that. You are wonderful . . . Oh—how selfish of me! It was *your* turn—I forgot all about you. You feel so huge inside me. Let's see if we can do nice things for you."

She pushed upward until she was sitting, his cock, still inside her. She leaned backward until Spur groaned, then began to weave forward and back, and to lift up and down in wildly erotic movements that tore Spur apart. He knew he couldn't stand it much longer. Another series of the rotations and he knew the time had come. He thrust up at her and lifted her into the air. His hips gave one last powerful thrust and he collapsed. She lowered herself on top of him, cushioning her breasts on his chest and kissing away the sweat from his forehead as Spur lay there panting, gulping in a torrent of air to revive his drained body.

All at once she wanted to talk. She began pouring out all of her troubles to him. Spur could barely listen, drained as he was, but he tried to follow it.

" . . . So I told him that of course I loved him and I wanted him, and I took my dress off and tried to entice him, but he ran out the door and I was so crushed that I had to go lie down. Then I did a sinful thing. I mean, I touched myself . . . down below . . . I rubbed and rubbed and it felt so good. I know I shouldn't have, but I was so crushed and so furious with Neil. Do you ever do that?"

"Do what?" asked Spur groggily.

"You know, *pretend* you're with someone."

"Everyone does, don't worry about it," he told her.

"Everyone? Even at *my* age?"

"And even much older than you." He put his arms around her. "How come you were able to come to my room? Where's your husband?" He realized he should have asked this before.

"He's on guard duty. Watch officer tonight."

"Oh. Then you can stay all night?"

"I never thought about it. Do you want me to?"

"You are a silly woman." He kissed both her breasts. "Yes, please stay."

And she did. Just before three in the morning, she got out of bed. Spur stood beside her and kissed her lips, then her nose and both eyes.

"Janet, you are a marvelous, beautiful woman. You make love deliciously, and any man alive would *kill* to spend one hour in bed with you. This unpleasantness will die down. Go back home and give Neil a little more time."

Janet giggled, reached down and patted his limp manhood. "I hope we didn't kill it."

"His nickname is Lazarus—he can rise from the dead." She laughed and he kissed her once more, then helped her put on her dress. She slipped out the back door into the night. Spur sighed and locked up after her. He stumbled back to bed and went to sleep at once. He didn't get up for breakfast. At 5:30 he awoke as usual, but turned over and went back to sleep. A man had to have some sleep, after all.

When Spur got up shortly before ten that morning, he wasn't sure what his next step was to be. He had been waiting for the bushwhacker to try again. He would follow up on the owners of the rifles. Both were enlisted men so that might make it easier to get the officer. There had to be an officer involved. He dressed in his uniform and walked around the post. Just before noon he was at the south end of camp where the rifle range had been set up. A different company was using it today. Lt. Omer Imhoff was the range officer. He barged up and down the line barking out orders as though he had been in the army for thirty years. Spur was surprised to see Lt. Casselberry there and discovered it was his company. Even though Neil had been on duty all night, he had come out with his troops.

Spur stood with the two officers for a moment, just in time to hear what must have been the final thrust of a series of teasing remarks.

"Casselberry, I hear you're going to need a papoose board in another nine months for your new family."

The words were said jokingly, but underneath Spur recognized in Imhoff a real dislike, a need to wound.

Lt. Neil Casselberry exploded. He charged across the space between them and thundered a fist into the surprised Imhoff, who staggered backward. Casselberry was all over him, slamming one solid punch after another into Imhoff's face until the big officer crumbled into the dust.

"Nobody talks that way about my wife, you bastard!" Casselberry roared. He punctuated the remark with a solid kick at Imhoff's belly. "You say anything like that again and I'll kill you, believe me, Imhoff, I'll kill you!" He kicked the man again.

By that time Spur was running toward them. The troopers on the line stopped firing, and turned to watch the fight. Any fight was a treat, but one between officers was a rarity, something to write home about. Before Spur got there Imhoff bellowed, "You fucking idiot, it was a *joke!*"

"Nobody jokes about my wife!" Casselberry roared and kicked Imhoff a glancing blow on the side of his head. The big officer rolled over and lay still. Casselberry was aiming another kick when Spur charged into him, caught him around the chest and drove him away. Spur slapped Casselberry twice and the junior officer shook his head, his eyes still glazed with hatred.

"Casselberry, sit down, right there, and don't move until I order you to. Do you understand me?" Spur snapped.

Casselberry shook his head again, and the mists dissolved. He looked up and nodded. "Yes, sir."

Spur hurried back to Lt. Imhoff. A sergeant had turned him over and lifted his head out of the dirt. He was conscious, blinking and groaning. Spur knelt beside him.

"Good morning, Lieutenant. What's your name?"

"Name . . . name . . ." Imhoff mumbled. "Yeah, I've got a name. I even know your name . . . Jones, old Doctor Jones."

Spur told the sergeant to keep the officer down and sent for the doctor. He stood and looked at the forty men who had clustered around. Spur picked out another sergeant and told him to take the men back to their barracks. The party was over.

By the time the doctor arrived, only the four men remained.

Casselberry sat throwing small pebbles at a bush. The scowl on his face seemed formed in stone. Spur watched the doctor look over the line officer, then went and sat beside Casselberry.

"Had Imhoff been talking like that before I came?" Spur asked.

"For an hour, sir. I just got to the point where I couldn't stand it."

"That's no reason to stomp a man to death."

"I know. I went out of my head for a moment."

"Put that in your report. I'm sure there will be some kind of an inquiry. It all depends how badly you shook up Imhoff's brains."

They watched the doctor get Imhoff to his feet and walk him toward the small dispensary.

"At least I didn't kill him," Casselberry said.

"An incident like this isn't going to help disperse any rumors about your wife, you must know that. If you want to help her and your career, put a capper on your temper. Now you had better carry on with your normal duties."

"Yes, sir. Thank you, sir." Lt. Casselberry stood and marched back toward his company area.

Buffalo Kane sat in the shade of the last barracks near the south end of camp. He had been watching the target practice and had seen the two officers fight. It wasn't much of a fight, he decided. That Lt. Casselberry had got in a surprise punch, and then waded in like a bare knuckle champion and knocked Imoff on his ass.

Kane kept whittling on a twisted cottonwood root as Lt. Casselberry strode past. The young officer was in trouble. From the looks of things, Casselberry had lost his temper. Temper. That made Buffalo think. Temper and anger. Anger at the Indians, all Indians. It fit. Casselberry was known to be a spit-and-polish, by-the-book officer. That kind always wants to impress his fellow officers and his superiors. Wiping out an Indian family might just help do it. Buffalo Kane went on whittling what looked like a wooden knife. He didn't even look up as Casselberry walked by, but he was thinking, could Lt. Neil Casselberry be his man?

# CHAPTER NINE

Spur McCoy was hungry for dinner that noon. He noticed that Lt. Imhoff wasn't there. That whole business could get nasty depending how Major Rutherford handled it. No, the major would understand the situation, and since Imhoff was the bigger man physically, he wouldn't want it on the official record that he had been beaten up by Casselberry. The outfall there would feed the rumor mongers. Janet would suffer in the long run.

The dinner was one long conversation about the fight that morning. Everyone in camp knew exactly what had happened and why. Most of them were cheering Lt. Casselberry.

"That Imhoff can be a real pain in the butt," Lt. Pauley said. "I've had a run-in or two with him. But, hell, he's young. Give him five years out here and he'll shape up."

"If he lives that long," Captain Grove, the adjutant, said.

No one asked Spur specifically what had happened, and for that he was thankful. Rank had certain privileges, even if the eagles were only flying temporarily.

After the meal Spur talked to the sergeant major and found out where the two men were who had the Henry rifles. One was on stable duty and the second was on a day-long patrol that had left just before dawn.

Spur found the first soldier, Private Hargrove. The young man was tall and lean, had a Texas accent and had been in the army for only two months. He was petrified to be talking to an officer, let alone a full colonel. All he could do was stare at the eagles. Spur wasn't about to tell him to relax and throw away a free advantage.

"Soldier, this is a part of my survey of this camp. One thing we're interested in is the Henry repeating rifle. The commissioner is interested in standardizing our arms. We want everyone to have the same make and caliber of rifle or carbine so it will make it easier on supply, and better tactically in the field. Do you think the Henry repeating rifle should be considered as the standard army weapon?"

"Uh, nope. I surely don't, Colonel."

"Why?"

"Well this 'un weapon of mine, say. It's nigh four feet long. No way to carry it comfortable on a horse. Scabbard too damn short, can't carry it across the saddle. Hail, 'bout the only thing a body can do is carry the damn thing in the crook of your arm. Fine for a couple miles, but forty miles a day and beans don't cut hay, Colonel."

"Is it accurate? Can you hit anything with it?"

"Hail, yes, sir. Got me the best shot in my company. 'Course I done some shooting down home. But my Henry will outshoot any of them other army rifles. Onlyest trouble is a body got to get the blamed thing to where you aim to use it."

"Do you have your weapon with you, Private Hargrove?"

"No, sir. Back at the barracks."

"Go back to your barracks and give your Henry to Corporal Kramer at supply. I need to inspect it. He'll issue you a temporary weapon."

"Now?"

"Right now, Private!"

Spur watched the gangling youth running for his barracks. Spur intended to eject some rounds from the two weapons and see if the extractor marks on the brass matched. A weapons expert in St. Louis said each extractor left a mark that was unique, and that any casing could be mated up with the gun it was fired from.

Spur went to the barracks where the second soldier with the Henry bunked. The barracks was a showplace, with neat bunks along each long wall. It was a spacious building with a high ceiling, windows every ten feet, and the bunks all had thick mattresses and blankets. In front of each bunk was a footlocker. A stove every twenty feet down the center provided heat. Three circular rifle racks stood in the center aisle with the polished weapons at the ready. A barracks orderly on duty tripped and almost fell when he saw the colonel, quickly got up and saluted.

"Soldier, which bunk belongs to Private Vuylsteke?"

"The middle . . . down in . . . Can I show you, sir?"

Spur nodded and the soldier tripped again but this

time kept his feet under him. Vuylsteke's bunk was the eighth one in from the end.

"He's on a patrol, I assume. Did he take his Henry rifle?"

"Don't know, sir—oh, no sir, he didn't take it. It's the long one in the rifle rack."

"Bring it here, Private."

The man ran for the rack, opened it and took out the long repeating rifle. He brought it back and gave it to the officer.

"I need to inspect this weapon, soldier. I'll give you a temporary receipt for it. If Vuylsteke needs another weapon he can sign out for one at the supply room." Spur handed the bewildered trooper a slip of paper with a short note and McCoy's signature.

Ten minutes later Spur was on the rifle range with Corporal Balder and the three Henry rifles. Spur fired three rounds from the first weapon and put a slip of paper with the cartridge cases with the serial number of the weapon. He put the brass and the paper in one pocket, then fired the other two rifles. Back in the supply room he laid out the brass with the slips of paper and compared them with cartridges from the bushwhacker's weapon. Spur used the largest magnifying glass he could find on post, and compared the scratches on the casings made by the extractor. Each was distinctive. Not even all three from the unknown gun matched each other, but there was a certain pattern they followed.

He studied each cartridge casing separately. Vuylsteke's gun could not possibly have fired the rounds. The next weapon was from the stable hand. Anyone could have stolen the Henry, used it and put it back. But the second set of brass did not meet the test. He checked the rifle that had been in the supply room. To Spur's surprise its cartridge cases matched the rounds exactly.

Whoever fired at him had taken the Henry from the supply room, used it, cleaned it and put it back before it was missed. Could it have been Corporal Kramer? Not likely.

He was back to step one of his journey, without a solid clue to work on. He kept going over the factors. Stolen army guns were turning up in Sioux hands; the raid on Buffalo Kane's shack and the murder of his family; the bushwhacking done by someone the first day he had arrived. Something else niggled at his mind—then he had it. The hammered gold trinket that belonged to Walking Fawn and had shown up later in the sutler's store bartered for some drinks.

Spur didn't know if any of it tied together. He wasn't even sure that the rifles were coming from this installation. But the fact that there were five rifles missing, gave him his only strong lead to this camp. He needed more facts, more hard intelligence about both sides of the trade. Which Indians were in on this?

Corporal Kramer stood at the door to the room where Spur had compared the casings.

"Corporal, could I talk with you a minute?" Spur asked.

The supply man came in and closed the door.

"This is all confidential, Kramer. I don't want anyone to know I've been comparing shell casings and extractor marks. This is just between us. It's important. Also, I need to know who has access to the supply room nights when you're not here."

"The Officer of the Guard has all the keys. I guess he could get in."

"Thank you, Corporal. If you would return these two weapons to the men I would appreciate it."

"Yes, sir!"

Spur walked slowly as he left the supply room and headed across the compound toward camp headquarters. The idea had come a few hours ago, and now it seemed more realistic. He had to get into the Black Hills. He had to watch the Indians, to see what they were up to. Nice work if you could do it without getting scalped.

He pushed into the outer office and was ushered into Colonel Underhill's quarters. The colonel was smoking a cigar, and Spur fished a crooked black one from his pocket and lit it.

"Underhill, I've got a problem. There is no chance I can identify the man who tried to shoot me. I need more information. As I understand it, the hostiles attack and retreat into the Black Hills. I've got to go in there and see what I can find out. I'm trying to solve this puzzle with only half the pieces."

Underhill took a long drag on his stogie, and blew the smoke halfway across the room. "Ordinarily I'd say what you suggest was suicide. But lately most of the Sioux have quieted down. We get a lot of Teton Sioux and Yankton Sioux around here, depending where the best hunting is. We haven't had any real trouble in two or three weeks. Might just be in between some tribal meets or pow-wows of some kind. I'll give you three good men and if you travel at night and stay hid during the day, you should make it."

"No men. I'll go alone. I can hide my trail and myself easier that way. I've been in Indian territory before, Colonel. All I'll need are some supplies and some weapons. I'd also like a dozen sticks of dynamite and caps and fuses. Never can tell when they might come in handy. Oh, I'd like a pound of sixpenny nails too, and some kind of sticky tape."

Colonel Underhill stared at Spur for a minute, then nodded. "You're welcome to all the supplies you want. But I'd appreciate it if you'd leave me a signed statement that you're going in alone, that I offered you an escort, and why you're going in. It might be handy to have when the board of inquiry arrives just in case you don't come back from the Black Hills."

Spur shrugged. "No problem. I'll have it ready before I go. Might as well get started today, get used to traveling at night."

Spur turned and walked out of the room and directly to the stables where he checked out the bay he had been riding. She was sleek and well fed, had been brushed down daily and exercised.

Back at his quarters he sorted through the equipment he had brought along. Most of it he rejected as too heavy. He would have no pack horse, just his own mount with saddle bags and a sack of food and gear. He selected carefully. Then he went to supply and drew a second pistol, a Remington new model army revolver and fifty rounds for it. At the mess hall he took exactly what he figured he would need for the six day ride including beans, coffee, two loaves of bread and some salt beef. At last he put in four tins of beef and a can of peaches. Two meals a day would be more than enough. He had everything put in a snap-top canvas bag. He then went to the

103

ammunition magazine to pick up the dynamite and chose six sticks that looked stable, carefully cut them in half with his knife and fused each one with a six-inch fuse. He would put the blasting caps on later. Out here you never knew when a hand bomb like these would come in handy.

Back at his quarters, Spur had his mount brought around and watched as two men loaded on his provisions. It was nearly three in the afternoon. He would have plenty of time to move well away from the camp before nightfall. Then he could practice his night travel. It had been some time.

Colonel Underhill stood on the porch of his head-quarters and watched as Spur rode over and gave him a sealed envelope.

"This is what you wanted, Colonel. I promise that you won't need it. I'll be back in seven days, unless I find something worthwhile. Then it may take me two days longer."

"Good luck—you're going to need it."

Spur waved and rode out the front gate and angled north. He crossed the White River and using a hand compass headed for a butte on the skyline that he should be able to identify for two hours after the sun went down. He rode at a gentle canter for the first two miles, then let the bay slow to a walk. Once he turned and watched the trail behind him. There was no reason that Underhill would send a patrol to follow him, but a man in his condition wasn't very reliable. Spur watched his backtrail for ten minutes from the far side of a rise, but could detect no movement.

Spur rode through a seemingly endless grassland, cut here and there by rivers and gullies. But the flatness of the Great Plains was both exciting and deadly. He angled a little more to the west to take advantage of a long valley leading to some low bluffs on the skyline.

It was dark before he reached the bluffs. Spur spotted a clump of willow and scrub with one cottonwood at the edge of the valley where some wet-weather feeder stream evidently came in. A half hour later he eased into the area, checked it thoroughly for any visiting Sioux hunters, and then relaxed. The Sioux must all be in their favorite hunting grounds to the north and west. He wouldn't worry about Indians for another two days.

Spur loose-tied his bay, fed her a quart of oats and let her drink at the tiny stream. Then he made camp. It was what he called a fast camp. McCoy took from the supply sack only what he needed, left the horse saddled and the sack in place, and only loosened the cinch strap. He could be in the saddle and moving within a minute of any sign of trouble.

Spur spread out his two blankets and searched the dry stream bed for some small, dry sticks. They would make a nearly smokeless fire for his coffee. He didn't mind missing a meal or two now and then, but coffee was a necessity. He made the fire and brewed his java in a tin can and at once put out the fire.

Spur sat back, letting the blackness close in on him again. He noticed a star or two through the thin canopy of leaves overhead. He hadn't seen a settler's cabin all day. He was out beyond the limits of the Nebraska pioneers. In fact he wasn't sure if he had crossed the line into Dakota Territory. The chances of finding friendly faces in the Dakotas were even smaller. He might not see anyone but Indians until he got back to the fort.

Spur lay on his blankets on his back, then leaned up on his elbow a moment to check his bay. She was moving around as if something was bothering her.

Suddenly something flashed in front of his eyes and he felt the cold steel of a knife blade pressing against his throat. Spur tensed. The knife was poised to slash across his windpipe. He was totally at the mercy of his unknown assailant.

# CHAPTER TEN

McCoy felt the knife pressure on his throat increase. He had not heard a thing, nor seen a movement. All he could do was talk.

"Hold on now, whoever you are. Don't do anything sudden or rash. I can't reach my weapon. If you can understand English, I hope you realize I'm not coming here to hurt anyone."

Spur felt movement behind him, and heard a soft sound that wasn't a word.

"Listen, I'm just passing through. I won't harm your lands. I'm not a scout for the army. I come in peace."

As quickly as it came, the knife was removed from his throat and he heard a laugh behind him, high bubbling feminine laughter that trailed off as he sat up and spun around, his hand clawing for the M & H .44 at his side.

"Colonel McCoy, you won't need your weapon. I won't hurt you—I came to help you."

He couldn't see through the murky darkness but

he recognized the voice. Spur relaxed and now it was his turn to laugh.

"Chitsa, welcome to Dakota Territory."

"We can have a campfire if you like. There isn't a Sioux within twenty miles of us."

"Why are you here, Chitsa?"

"I told you, to help you. If I let you go into the Black Hills alone, you will be caught, tortured and killed. I don't want that to happen." She paused. "Wait a moment, I'll relight the fire, and if your grounds are still good, could we brew another cup? I'm very fond of coffee."

Spur turned and lay forward on his blankets as he watched the small dark shadow moving near where his fire had been. Sooner than he expected the fire blazed up. Chitsa brought more wood and built it up so it lighted the small campsite.

Chitsa sat in front of him on the ground and he saw that she wore a one piece doeskin Indian dress tied at the waist with a leather thong, and moccasins. She smiled at him.

"Do not try to send me back. You are going into dangerous areas. It is a foolish journey, but I can't sit by and let you die. It would be a great waste. We can ride out another day, camp in a place I know where there is sweet water, many berries and some wild fruit and rabbits. We can talk and I'll show you how Indians live, work, and play."

"No, Chitsa. I have a job to do, and it must be done."

"Then I must go with you. What exactly are you trying to find out on this fool's mission?"

Spur laughed and she smiled. "You have a delicate way with words, Chitsa. I may just tie you up and leave you beside a tall tree until I return."

"You would have to catch me first. And remember how I slipped up on you even when you were quietly listening. I am an Indian, Spur. I can take you places so the Sioux will never know we have been there. But I must know what you wish to discover."

He told her his mission, then, quickly and simply. Her eyes grew cold, and her fists tightened.

"I am an Indian, but I have been educated by white men. I am a woman in two camps. I detest whoever is selling the rifles to the Sioux. Although they are not my tribe, they will die like buffalo being driven over a cliff. I will help you find out what you need to know."

Spur thought about it. She could be a tremendous asset in the next few days—and a great temptation. He decided to avoid that issue for now.

"Chitsa, if you come with me it may help. I need to find out which group of Sioux are buying the guns and I need to know who among them has contact with the insider at Camp Sheridan. I also need to know what schedule or method of payment has been made."

She thought about it, her round face serious now, her almond-shaped eyes showing worried. "Most of what you seek will be impossible to find out. But we can learn some of it. We must be cautious. After to-morrow we will travel only at night, and we must not light a fire once we reach the land of the Sioux."

"A question. At lunch the other day you looked like a fashionable, civilized young lady. How have you kept your worlds intact? Have you learned Indian skills so you could be comfortable in both camps?"

She smiled at him. "Grace Underhill said I had been with them for fifteen years. She exaggerates. It's been ten years. I am now twenty-one. I had eleven years to learn Indian ways. My tribe was the Shawnee and we learned to live with the white man quickly, but still we never abandoned our Indian heritage.

"Even now I get restless. Grace knows it and pretends it doesn't happen. I go out into the prairie, and live as the Indians do. I am sometimes gone for a day, sometimes a week. One summer I stayed away for a month, and Grace was ill with worry when I went back. I can live off the land. I can provide my own food and clothing if necessary."

"Remarkable. So you think my mission is stupid and that we should go back?"

"You should have consulted me before you planned it. We may be able to find out some things you need to know. Yes, it will be productive to continue."

"How? Do you have a horse?"

"Of course. Your bay sniffed her out—that's what almost gave me away."

"Now there is one other matter," Spur said, staring at her. The loose fitting garment totally hid her figure, but he had a powerful imagination.

"Spur McCoy, I'm just as interested in that 'other matter' as you are. But first we must see what information we can find to stop the sale of the rifles. That is much more important. Then we will discuss my virginity, and how and when you will instruct me in making love for the first time."

Spur sat back, astonishment washing over him.

"How did you know that was what I was talking about?"

"I am woman, and an Indian. I could tell. There is an old Shawnee custom that allows any Indian girl unmarried by the time she is eighteen to choose the man who will pierce her maidenhead. The selected male does not have the right to refuse—and usually he does not wish to refuse."

"Is that a real custom, or have you created it especially for your own situation?"

"If I could create plots like that, Mr. McCoy, I would be a great novelist or write plays to rival Shakespeare."

"You just might be good at it! But you're right about one thing. If we're risking our lives out here, we better not worry about anything else until we get back."

"From now until then, I will be your sister, your guide, your scout and your advisor. If I need to bathe in a stream, you will stand guard and look the other way, and you will not intrude on my privacy. Now we should sleep. We will make much better time tomorrow than you did today. Do you realize that you had to backtrack twice today to get around bluffs you could have avoided?"

She stood gracefully, vanished out of the firelight for a few minutes and returned with her horse, an Indian Pinto pony with an army saddle, complete with .44 pistol and carbine in the boot. She took down a blanket roll and spread it beside his. Then she scooped dirt onto the fire with her hands and lay down on top of her blankets. Within minutes she was sleeping, lying on her back, with one hand across her stomach and the other above her head.

Spur watched her in the pale, filtered moonlight. She was his sister. She was also a combination of Indian and white that would surely get her in trouble sooner or later. San Francisco would be a good place for her. She'd be a sensation . . . He shook his head. Sleep—what he needed was sleep. He drifted off and dreamed of finding a secret cache of rifles in boxes, but when he opened the boxes, the rifles turned into rattlesnakes and began striking at him.

He woke once, saw that Chitsa was still sleeping soundly, and dozed off again.

Spur awoke at 5:30 as usual. As soon as he sat up, Chitsa was awake and on her feet. Before he got up off the blanket she had the fire going and had started frying bacon and making flapjacks from her own supplies.

"This is the last civilized food for you," she said. "The eggs are from camp, in honor of your bravery —and foolhardiness. Eat this in good health."

Spur thought he knew all about camping and life on the trail, but in the next ten minutes the small Indian girl showed him that he was a total neophyte. She had everything packed and the horses ready to go before he had the sleep out of his eyes. She wore the same doeskin dress and rode her pony astride. She led the way, made a sudden turn to the left following the valley and headed for a cliff he was sure they would never be able to climb.

He asked her about it and she only smiled. Just as they came to it, Spur spotted a pass. While not more than two hundred feet high, going around the bluffs would have caused them a five mile detour.

"You do good scout work," Spur said.

"This is nothing. I know this country like my bedroom. I've been into the Black Hills twice while I have been here. Neither time did I let the Sioux know I was there. If they found me, they would take me prisoner."

By noon of the first full day they had passed Lone Butte and Spur could see a tower ahead that Chitsa said the Indians called Hay Canyon Butte. Several times that morning she had stopped, dismounted and stared into the distance, turning her head to catch the wind and testing the scents in the air. The last time she nodded and smiled.

"Come, we must hurry, I want to show you something."

They rode hard up a slight draw to a continuation of the monotonous plains. At the top she held up her hand to stop and they walked the horses cautiously so they could see over the waving grass.

Spur caught his breath. "Magnificent! I've never seen a better herd. But what are they doing here?"

Ahead of them on a gentle, rolling downslope were more than a hundred head of buffalo. The bulls stood nearly six feet tall, huge shaggy, angry-eyed creatures with short pointed horns and now almost bare hindquarters due to the summer shedding. A dozen or so bulls patroled the outer limits of the herd and the cows and spring calves grazed inside.

"You knew they were here," Spur said.

"Yes, of course. I'm Indian."

"You smelled them on the wind?"

"Partly. My senses are not sharpened yet. It usually takes me two or three days. Then I could have scented them from five miles away. These were less than a mile."

"But they are *downwind* from us."

"Yes. It is more than the scent, there is a *presence* with the buffalo. So many Indians rely totally upon them for their life. They use the meat, the hide, the horns, even the hooves. No part of a bison goes to waste in an Indian camp. We make buffalo robes when the big creatures have their full winter coat of long shaggy hair and the dense wooly undercoat. We make our teepees from the hides. We preserve the meat, dry it, pound it into pemmican. Many of the Plains Indians also worship the buffalo."

She frowned. "We must go."

"Why?"

"We go now because wherever there are this many buffalo at this time of year, there surely are Indians, scouts at least to keep track of the herd. It is the right number for a medium-sized camp of Sioux to attack. Here they would start grass fires and drive the buffalo over the cliff. It's the easiest way for the braves to kill the beasts. Some of the big bulls weigh more than 2200 pounds. Even the cows can weigh 1200 pounds."

She turned her horse and rode at right angles to the herd, which did not see them, and soon they were into a draw that led in the direction they needed to go.

He came abreast of her. "It's a little unusual to see that many buffalo together this time of year," she said. "We're right in the middle of the calving season. Usually they wander around in bands of eight or ten with their newborn calves. Come August it will be breeding or 'running' season and the males become restless. Fights between the bulls is common and the small bands merge into giant herds that often go as high as five thousand. The bellowing and bawling of that many buffalo keeps everyone awake for miles around."

"And the Sioux live off the buffalo which means we need to get away from them," Spur said. "Makes sense."

They stopped near sunset. There had been no noon break, and Spur figured they had covered over forty miles. Chitsa picked out the campsite, a dense growth of willow and chokecherry bordering a small trickle of a stream. Behind the willow a sandstone cliff rose thirty feet.

"Not even an Indian could sneak up on us here," she said.

Chitsa decided that they could risk a small fire for coffee, but only if she gathered the materials. She prowled the almost dry stream bed for half an hour and came back with her hands full of dry sticks. She showed him how to find branches that had been weathered, soaked and dried for years until they had most of the sap drained out of them. She prepared everything, then lit the fire and Spur soon watched the coffee boil over the smokeless flames.

"After any smoke gets through the willow leaves, it will be washed nearly clean," she said. "Even the best Sioux hunter would need to be within 200 yards of us to smell this smoke."

They had coffee, some slabs of cheese with the bread he had brought and he opened a tin of the beef. She heated it on the coals of the fire and then built up the fire enough to boil more coffee.

"We won't eat this well for several days," she warned him.

It soon grew dark and they let the fire die down and go out. Spur watched her in the moonlight. She was like a wraith, a ghost dancer, and at the same time more educated than most white women. She was truly Woman of Two Camps. She had put up her long twin braids in a bun at the back of her neck so they would be out of the way. The soft doeskin dress clung to her now, showing the swell of her breasts.

She turned and found him staring and she smiled. "Not yet, Colonel. Remember that must wait until after we spy on the mighty Sioux." There was a smile wreathing her face as she went on, "Now, which of Shakespeare's plays were his greatest? Would you say *King Lear, Macbeth* or perhaps *Hamlet?*"

She watched him and Spur chuckled. "You caught me. But as far as the bard goes, I have no favorite, although *The Merchant of Venice* does hold a warm spot in my heart."

"I might have known." She smiled. "Now, Colonel, if the beast in you is corraled, we should be sleeping. When midnight comes we'll be up and moving again until dawn. We travel only at night from now on. Do you trust my scouting?"

"So far, fine. I'll wait until we're back before I give a final evaluation. If we don't both get back alive, you fail."

"Sleep time, Colonel."

Spur woke promptly at midnight as he had instructed his mental alarm clock to do, but Chitsa was already up and had both horses ready.

An hour later Spur was amazed at the way the small Indian girl maneuvered her mount through

116

the Dakota plains, and how well she kept them on a northwesterly route. They made good time and he figured they had covered another twenty miles as it began to get light. They entered a small valley with a heavy stand of cottonwoods and got inside the woods just as the first streaks of dawn tinged the eastern sky.

Once beneath the trees, Chitsa stopped her mount and sat motionless, signalling Spur to do the same.

She pointed ahead and Spur listened. A murmur of voices came through the morning stillness. Chitsa slid off her mount, handed the reins to Spur and vanished into the woods without a sound. They had agreed that any chance happening of a Sioux war party or even a two or three-man hunting group meant they had to dissolve. If they were seen they would be hunted down and killed. If they saw the Indians first they would attempt to stay unobserved. Now his scout and new friend was walking toward the Indian camp.

She was back in less than a minute, holding up two fingers, and drawing an imaginary bow. Two hunters. Spur slid off his bay, pulled out his Spencer repeater and made sure a round was in the chamber and the safety off. They both held the muzzles of their mounts so the sensitive nostrils would not pick up the scent of the Indian horses and reveal their presence.

As they stood there waiting for the Sioux to leave and continue their hunt, one Indian rode past the cottonwood brush and directly into them. The Sioux carried his bow in his right hand, ready for any game. When he saw the two horses, he notched an arrow and had it half drawn when Spur fired the

Spencer. The slug caught the rider in the throat and tore out half his windpipe and a section of his spinal column. The dead brave jolted backward off the horse which kept going, pounding past them.

Even before the rifle shot sound had started echoing, Chitsa was running toward the camp they had just left. Spur ran with her, crashing through the brush while she moved soundlessly. The girl stopped behind a tree. He halted behind a cottonwood and looked toward where he figured the camp should be. Spur saw nothing but more brush. Then something moved. He watched again. To the right, away from the camp, the movement came once more and he made out the form of a lurking Indian, drawing a bow. The arrow was aimed at Chitsa.

Without aiming, Spur jerked the Spencer around and fired the long gun from his hip. The Indian screamed in pain and fury, slammed against a tree and slid downward, dead by the time he hit the ground.

The shot's crashing roar faded slowly, and when it was gone, so was Chitsa. He saw her a moment later twenty feet ahead, then farther toward the camp. Spur followed her cautiously, making sure no more redskins lurked in the brush. He remembered her two fingers, but there might be another Indian or two away from camp.

Five minutes later he came from in back of a huge cottonwood and saw the remains of a small cooking fire. Over it lay a rabbit on a spit. One Indian pony stepped nervously where it had been ground-tied.

Chitsa returned to the camp and stared at Spur for several seconds. Then she walked up to him, loosened the tie at her waist and pulled the doeskin

118

dress over her head. She folded it and knelt on it in front of Spur. He was amazed at the perfection of her body. Her breasts were small, darkly nippled and with almost no areolas. Her waist was narrow and the black fur at her crotch was luxuriant.

"Most honored one," she said softly, her eyes downcast in respect. "Most skillful and brave one who has this day saved my life, I humbly submit to your every wish. All previous agreements are canceled." She looked up at him in admiration. "I was truly a dead woman. I saw death in the eyes of the Sioux at the same time your bullet struck him. It was my own death I saw. My life now belongs to you, Colonel McCoy. I am yours in body and mind. Each waking minute of my life from now until I die will be at your service, since I no longer have a life of my own to live."

She stood and put her arms around him, pressing close. "I am yours to command. The hunting party was only two. One was rushing somewhere, perhaps with a message about the herd of buffalo. The other came when your shot alerted him. We are safe for now. No other Sioux warriors are in this area."

Spur bent and kissed her cheek.

"My little sister is still my little sister. Now dress quickly and let's find out if the rabbit is cooked."

A flash of relief covered her face for a second, then she turned, pulled on the dress, tied the belt and checked the rabbit. She built up the fire with dry twigs and by the time Spur had brought up their horses, the meat was cooked.

They ate it hungrily, licking the bones clean, then washing their hands in the small stream.

"We must not stay here," she said. "The spirits of

the two Sioux warriors will not let us rest."

They mounted and rode to the northern edge of the brush, and she studied the scene.

"The valley goes north and east. It will be an hour's ride to that green spot by the bluff. We should be unseen this early."

Spur watched her small round face critically.

"You say 'shouldn't,' but what if we are? What if a larger hunting party is coming? What if a lone warrior spots us and spreads the word?"

"Then we will ride like the wind, use our rifles and our pistols and when the night comes we will hide ourselves and escape. We *shall* return from this patrol. I know. I saw it in the stars last night." She frowned. "I am Indian—I can read the sign."

"But you are afraid of two dead Sioux."

A frown touched her face. "Do not joke about the spirits. I will go now. Either go with me or stay here —it's up to you."

# CHAPTER ELEVEN

Spur let the Indian maiden ride a hundred yards alone. She never looked back. Then he dug his heels into the bay and caught up to Chitsa, riding alongside. She urged her horse faster and they cantered the two miles to the spot below the bluff and checked the woods carefully. There were no overnight visitors there ahead of them.

"You knew I'd come with you."

"Of course. You're a logical man. And right now you need what I know, you need me to help you. I'll need you later. I'll need you then very much." She was serious as she said it, then turned away and picked out the best spot to hide the horses. They took their sleeping blankets and nestled down in some thick brush toward the back of the woodsy area. Spur stretched out and she put her blankets beside him, rolled toward him and snuggled against his side.

"Now we sleep," she said and closed her eyes.

Spur woke up around noon. He felt the girl move

beside him. She had one arm thrown over his chest, then she smiled in her sleep and turned the other way. Spur stood and checked the area. The horses were still where they had been tied, and quiet. He went to the edge of the trees but saw no movement in the long valley.

When he lay down on the blankets her head searched for him, found his shoulder and she smiled, moved closer to him and returned to her deep sleep.

Spur woke again at five that afternoon. Chitsa was not beside him. He checked the horses and she was not there. A twinge of fear touched him. He went to the stream and found her kneeling beside it. She had shed her dress and was washing. He stopped, embarrassed, afraid of offending her.

"It's all right, Colonel. Don't be shy—you and I have no secrets. Bathing is good for the body." She had spoken without turning around and he saw only her brown back where she knelt. Now she stood and turned. She was naked, holding a small cloth at her face, drying it. Her light tan skin glowed and she was the most naturally beautiful woman he had ever seen. Her small breasts bounced slightly as she bent and pulled on white cotton drawers, then a pair of brown men's pants she had cut down to fit. Over this she put the doeskin Indian dress.

"The trousers make it much easier to ride on the saddle," she explained. "Are you ready to eat?"

He had not seen nor smelled her fire, but it glowed red with coals as she led him to it. The can of coffee boiled gently and there were slabs of bread spread with crabapple jelly. As they ate and drank the strong coffee, he caught her attention.

"Chitsa, you weren't serious about that slave-for-life story you gave me, were you?"

"Of course I meant it. I am Indian!" There was pride and a touch of anger in her voice.

"Well, uh. . . . We're going to have to talk about that. You see, slavery has been abolished. It's against the law."

"I will be a love slave, that's different."

"We'll talk about that back at Camp Sheridan," said Spur, feeling distinctly uncomfortable.

"I will not be able to be your sister much longer, either. I have these feelings when I touch you, even when I'm sleeping."

"Later. It will be dark soon. How far are we from the Black Hills?" he asked.

"We have been in them for half a day. The section we are heading for is another day's ride north. But there could be camps of Sioux hunters anywhere through this area. We must be cautious."

Ten minutes later it was dark and they were moving out of the patch of woods and into the valley. They angled past a mountain on the left and moved up another valley, went to the ridgeline and there Chitsa stopped and looked to the north.

"Smell the smoke?" she asked.

Spur shook his head.

"Four or five miles ahead. A big campfire. Probably a hunting party roasting buffalo steaks and skinning the kill. Let's go have a look."

He started to stop her but shrugged. Any Sioux he saw might provide information, especially if he had rifles. He followed her, watching how straight she sat on the horse, and he wondered what it would

be like to make love to her. Young, tender and un-
tried. She would be an exciting experience, he knew,
and he was starting to look forward to it—but not
yet, not while the threat of a Sioux tomahawk loom-
ed over them.

An hour later they had left their horses and faded
from one tree to the next as they worked their way
up a hill concealed by its welcome growth of young
pine toward the Indian camp.

After another hundred yards, Chitsa lay down on
her stomach and crawled the last fifteen feet to the
brow of the ridge. Below them a huge campfire blazed, sending sparks and smoke high into the air and
lighting up the gully like noontime.

To one side, squaws worked skinning out two
huge buffalo. They quartered one animal, lay the
slabs on the skins and cut them into portions for the
various family units, then some squaws joined the
braves around the fire. Someone had a bottle of fire-
water. It went the rounds. The braves grew more
boisterous. A rifle shot slammed through the peaceful silence, and Spur turned his head quickly to find
the shooter. The man stood to one side, his posture
showing the effects of the strong drink. Two braves
grabbed the man, grabbed the weapon away from
him and pushed him back to the circle around the
fire.

"Twelve braves, a small band," Chitsa said.
"They killed two bison, probably with the rifle.
They butchered them where they fell, and made
their camp here. They will treat the skins, dry the
meat, eat until they almost burst, and then move on
to wherever they were headed when their scout

found the buffalo. Everything stops when buffalo are sighted during hunting season."

Spur listened. He wished he had brought a better pair of binoculars. With the army issue, he was able to pick up some details of the rifle, but not enough. It was either an old Sharps, or a Spencer repeater. Either one would be deadly in the hands of an Indian who had taken the time to learn to use it. More and more Indian chiefs now wanted rifles. The "firesticks" at first were laughed at because they belched their fire so slowly. A tomahawk could be swung forty dozen times while a soldier reloaded the old muskets once with ball and powder. Cartridge rifles were better.

"How long will they stay here?" Spur asked.

"It depends how much whiskey they have. The squaws will be finished with their duties in three or four days, depending how thin they cut the meat to dry, and some of the braves will be drunk for three or four days."

"Do you see any more rifles?"

"Yes—the brave at the center of the group around the fire. He could be some kind of sub-chief."

Spur turned his glasses there. The Indian was holding a Sharps, a powerful long-range weapon that came in several calibers and was highly accurate. Two rifles, two buffalo. He wondered how many settlers those same guns had killed.

Chitsa motioned him to move back and when they were safely into the woods she touched his arm.

"We should be leaving this place. I have bad feelings about it. No sign, but some evil thing is here. I don't like it. The spirits are not pleased."

They walked to their horses, made a wide detour around the camp and pushed on north along a ridgeline that kept moving higher and higher. Just after two in the morning by Spur's Waterbury pocket watch, they stopped.

"We can't go much farther before I have a chance to look around in the daylight. So tell me exactly what you want to see," she said.

"I want to find two or three camps, maybe an abandoned campsite. I want to learn if every band has guns, or only a few. And I want to see if there is any move toward making war on the whites."

"That is possible. Now we will sleep and in the morning I'll find some villages we can spy on."

They found a small ravine clogged with young pine trees, a dozen larger ones and a smattering of brush that would hide the horses. The end of the canyon sloped up into a rock wall and below it the brush was thick. Chitsa hummed a little tune as she spread out the blankets, then took one and using pointed sticks turned the blanket into a wall masking them from the downstream side. She took a candle from her supplies and lit it. It made a surprisingly strong light after the darkness. She sat on the blanket.

"Now, Spur McCoy. Now I want you to make love to me." She smiled at his expression. "Yes, we are safe here. The Sioux are not making war. Hunters do not roam this land at night, and no travelers would come past this area. Even if they were, it would be only blind luck for one to stumble on us. I have waited many, many summers for this moment. Please help me."

Spur sat beside her, reached down and kissed her

cheek, then turned her pretty face and kissed her trembling lips. Gone was her sense of control, her sureness. Now she was on uncharted waters.

Chitsa made a small mewing sound in her throat. Her hand came up and touched his cheek, then she parted her lips and let his tongue probe inside. His arms came around her and she whimpered softly, her small hands clinging to his shirtfront as the kiss continued. When it ended she smiled up at him in the candle glow.

"Kissing. Yes, I like kissing. Especially that kind. Could we try it again?"

Her arms went around him this time and she held him tightly. He let her tongue explore this time and she made the small sounds again. He broke off the kiss and leaned away so he could touch her breast through the soft doeskin. She looked up at him in wonder.

"Yes, I *want* you to touch me there. I've never thought about it before, but it's a very pleasant sensation."

Both his hands cupped her breasts and he caressed them gently, then he slid one hand under her dress and upward to her left breast. When his hand touched her bare flesh, she sighed, "Yes, yes! That is nice. I heard two women talk about it once. Yes, it feels delicious. May I take this off?"

He helped her lift the doeskin over her head and he marveled again at her small round breasts and their dark nipples. He touched them again, playing with them, watching her reaction of surprise, then acceptance, and saw her desire building.

"Breasts are the most beautiful part of a woman, did you know that, Chitsa? So perfectly round, so symmetrical, so delightfully tipped, and so good tasting!''

He bent and kissed one of her breasts and she jumped in surprise. Her glance darted to his face and then her expression mellowed. He kissed her breast again, then licked her nipple and she sighed.

"That's nice, Spur, so nice."

He licked her again and then nibbled at her dark nipple which had sprung up almost doubling its size.

"Suddenly the night air is quite warm," she said, smiling mischievously at him.

Spur finished with one breast and moved to the other one, where his ministrations brought a low moan from Chitsa.

"Spur—beautiful man—I hope you're not in a rush. I would like you to nibble on me that way for an hour."

"We have better things to do," he said, taking off his boots, and sliding down his pants. He pulled off his shirt and smiled at her. She was tense, pensive, but Spur kissed away her doubts, and then slid off his underpants.

"Great Spirits!" she said, staring at his erection. "Huge—it's so big—I never dreamed . . . You don't mean that huge thing is supposed to go inside . . ." She stopped, her hand over her mouth.

Spur moved closer, picked up her other hand and moved it to his thigh. "Go ahead, look at me. Touch me, nothing down there will break. Go ahead."

Her expression changed and she was like a little girl with a new toy. She touched him, grasped his manhood, bent it back and forth, then moved lower to Spur's heavy scrotum and the forest of reddish hair.

She looked up. "I'm not hurting him?"

Spur chuckled. "Lazarus doesn't mind at all. You're going to be very good friends with him."

She moved Spur around, inspecting him thoroughly, but was most fascinated by his penis.

Chitsa still wore her trousers. Spur reached for the buttons on the fly, but she moved his hands up to her breasts and leaned over to be kissed. Spur did, rubbing her breasts harder now as his tongue drove deeply into her mouth. As he kissed her, he pushed her down gently on her back, and moved his mouth to one breast, then unbuttoned her trousers as she moaned softly beneath him.

When the fasteners were open, he pulled the pants off, then put his hand on the white material of the drawers and worked downward.

"Are you seducing me?" she asked, interested.

He kissed her, then put his hand on her crotch and felt a wet place through the thin cotton material. She gasped with delight and when he ended the kiss, he smiled.

"Of course I'm seducing you, which only means a little persuasion. The next time you won't need so much persuasion, and after that *you'll* probably be seducing *me!*"

She nodded and his mouth went back to her breast and his hand rubbed the damp spot. She moaned again and he sat up and put his fingers under the tops of her cotton drawers. She held his hands.

"Are you sure there will be room? I mean, he's so *large.*"

"Yes, sweet little Chitsa, there will be room, and it will be so delightful you'll want to stay this way all night." He bent and kissed her fingers. She let go of his hands and he pulled the fabric down slowly. For each inch he moved the white cloth, he kissed her hips and then her little belly, going around her thick black thatch, and kissed the cloth down her legs until the drawers came off her feet.

Her legs were tightly together. Spur put his hand on her fur and kissed her lips until she purred. Then his finger explored until he found the wet spot. He worked farther to find her tiny hard node and swiftly he rubbed it back and forth. Four times was all it took before Chitsa cried out in surprise as her body trembled with a short sharp series of vibrations that left her gasping.

When she recovered he kissed her gently. "That, small Indian Maiden, was a climax—your body giving you a thrill of the preliminaries to making love. It's even better during lovemaking. Did you like it?"

"Oh, yes, do it again!"

He did.

"So marvelous! So wonderful! Why didn't those women tell me how glorious that feels! Oh, no *wonder* they didn't tell me." She kissed him. "Now, what's next?"

He took her hand and closed it around his erection.

She shivered. "I *still* don't see how it's going to fit."

Spur kissed her, then spread her legs and moved his hand down and found her slit. He edged a finger into the wet, slippery place and Chitsa murmured with pleasure. He spread her juices around the outer lips, kissed her again, then knelt between her spread thighs.

"This is the most wonderful part," he said. He used his hand to coat the purpled head of his cock with saliva, then angled down and touched her sensitive outer lips with his staff.

She shivered. "Will it hurt?"

"It will feel so marvelous you'll not remember anything else."

He probed gently, was sure he was positioned, then increased the pressure a little at a time until he felt her muscles relax and he drove forward.

Chitsa yelped with a sudden, harsh pain. Then it was over and she realized that she was a woman—no longer an Indian maid—and tears filled her eyes as she moved her hips to meet his thrusts with a pleasure, a warmth, a womanly understanding that she had never known before. Total joy and possessiveness flowed from her and she was determined never to leave this man's side. She would be with him and be his woman forever and ever!

Spur let himself go. He felt primitive, like a male animal in final union with the female. He rooted and soared, he pounded forward into her slender form listening to the contented sounds she made as she accepted his plunging. He sensed her feet rising until her legs were in the air over his back and he powered again and again into her until sweat beaded his forehead. Spur erupted inside her five, six, then seven times in ecstatic spasms.

He lowered himself toward her then and kissed her lips gently.

"Oh, that was *beautiful!*" Chitsa said. "I've never felt so wanted, so needed, so loved!"

He shook his head, hearing her words but not quite sure what she was saying. He blinked, saw her face below him and bent and kissed her again, then eased down on her for just a moment. Her arms wrapped around him and pulled him lower. He let only part of his weight rest on her, and she smiled at him and nodded.

"Yes, I want you on top of me! I'll come with you —I'll go anywhere you want me to. After we find out about the rifles, and discover who is selling them, then I'll come with you to whatever army post you are assigned to. All I have to pack is my books."

Spur's mind unfroze and he recognized the meaning of her words. He tried to move gently away but she held him, still gasping after his exertion.

Chitsa listened to him and grinned. "You really got your steam boilers heated up! Did I do all right? I mean, I heard some of the women talking about 'satisfying' a man. Is that what I did? Did I satisfy you?"

He laughed, bent and kissed her and then pulled himself up, lifting away from her and sitting on the blanket beside her.

"Yes, small Indian maiden, you satisfied me. What about you? Were all those summers of waiting worth it?"

"Oh, yes! Yes! I loved it. The little hurt at first was over so fast, and then everything was perfect. Marvelous, wonderful, a feeling like nothing I've ever experienced before! Can we do it again?"

Spur chuckled. "The male of the species can't do it a dozen times in a row like you girls can. I need a little more time to recharge my energy."

"An hour?"

He nodded. "An hour will be fine."

She sat up suddenly and looked at his crotch. "I

want to see him all relaxed and soft. He *does* get soft, doesn't he? You couldn't ride around all day with that hard thing in your pants."

She found his penis and watched for a minute, then her curiosity satisfied, she turned.

"I'm hungry."

"Making love affects some people that way. But maybe we should get some sleep."

"First we'll eat the last of the cheese and some bread and then we'll make love again, and *then* we'll get some sleep," said Chitsa firmly.

# CHAPTER TWELVE

They both woke up at dawn. She reached up and kissed him. Her naked body slid half on top of him and her nipples tickled his chest.

"I wish we had time to make love again, right now, but we have to be moving." She sat up, pulled up her white drawers, then shook her head and took them off. She put on her doeskin dress, tied the rawhide and then touched her hair.

"It is too long and too clean. I must look like a Sioux squaw if they see me." She picked handfuls of dirt and rubbed it into her hair and into the braid, then rubbed more of the dirt on her face, arms and legs. She dug into her supplies and brought out a forked stick and a stained, dirty rawhide bag.

"I will be just another squaw digging for roots and searching for berries. Even the mighty Sioux braves like more to eat than bison meat."

"Your horse?"

"No. Indian women are not permitted to ride horses. The horse is the prize and the privilege of the brave. And you said slavery was outlawed!"

She ate the rest of the bread and some of the cold canned meat, then looked at the hills. "I'll go first to the ridgeline and see where I need to go and how I can get there. I'll stay in the pine timber as much as possible. And I won't be more than two or three miles away. You stay here and keep quiet and invisible. There shouldn't be anyone coming through here. The main trail leads well around this area. I should be back before noon."

Spur nodded and sat on the blanket cleaning his pistols. He worked on the Spencer repeating rifle as well, and soon had all three in perfect order. Chitsa had faded from the camp so silently that he didn't know when she left. She had taken down the blanket tent—it might attract attention.

He went to the horses, found a place he could walk them to water without being seen and let them drink, then ground-tied them in a hidden spot where they could find some graze. He would feed them the rest of the oats as soon as Chitsa came back.

Spur had wanted to go with her, but he realized she was right. Indian country was her element, not his. If he had blundered in here alone, it was possible that he might not have returned. That would have pleased Colonel Underhill.

With nothing to do, Spur grew restless. He checked the camp again. It was practically impossible to identify the area from even a few feet away. The heavier pine cover helped. It was a relief to move from the plains into the gentle foothills, then deeper into the Black Hills themselves. The sturdy pine trees began scrubby and short, then lifted taller and taller until in this place many were two feet thick and a hundred feet high.

Spur worked his way up the side of the ridge, staying undercover in the heavy growth. At the top he could see out both sides, including the valley they had come up last night, and another smaller valley. He checked both carefully for any movement. Nothing at all showed in the larger valley, but in the other one across the ridge he saw motion near the far end. Using his binoculars, Spur made out a small band of buffalo—one huge bull, five or six cows and several calves grazing peacefully.

Suddenly below him in the valley, a pair of horses bolted from the tree cover and raced across the grasslands. Spur felt a moment of panic, swung the glasses to the animals and saw that both were wild horses, a big black which might at one time have been an army mount, and a smaller Indian-type pony. Both were free and racing across the meadow just for the enjoyment of it.

Once more Spur quartered the valleys, searching for any sign of Indians. He found none, rolled on his back and had a half hour nap, then went below to the campsite.

Chitsa came back an hour later. She had stopped at the stream and scrubbed herself, and washed out her long black hair. She had combed it with her fingers, letting it dry in the sun. Chitsa slipped out of her doeskin dress and walked to Spur, all glistening, clean and lovely.

She knelt beside him and leaned over him. Spur caught one breast and kissed it. She purred in her throat and pushed him flat on his back.

"Please, darling Spur, make love to me right now!" she whispered.

Twice they made gentle love on the soft grass in the mountain meadow. Only afterwards did she tell him what she had found.

"Two miles from here is a good sized Sioux village. It looks like a hunting camp, and I'd say it's about ready to move. We can get there under cover all the way. No one will spot us. Everyone is working hard. The women are taking down dried buffalo strips, the braves are making arrows and feathering old ones, getting ready for another hunt. We can leave here just after midday and get there quickly. I did see one rifle."

"A hunting camp, not a war camp?"

"No, not with women and children, and pack horses to carry back the buffalo meat."

They had a quick lunch of cold canned meat and berries that she had found, then packed up and moved out. Chitsa led the way, and both walked their horses. Spur carried the repeating Spencer in his right hand with a round in the chamber ready to fire.

They wound up the valley in the edge of the timber, went over the crest and down the other side, then over two more ridges and left the horses in some dense timber. They moved slower going up the last ridge. Chitsa said the camp was just over the top.

They edged into some small pines growing on the ridgeline and could see the camp below. There was one tipi, and a fire. Spur guessed there were about thirty men and women working around the camp. The women were now packing dried buffalo meat in bundles made from buffalo hide.

To one side Spur saw the glint of sun off metal and found a tall Indian with a wide strip of hair running down the center of his scalp and wearing blue Cavalry pants. He was demonstrating how to load and fire the rifle. Spur studied the weapon through his binoculars. It was a Sharps single shot carbine. There were thousands of them still in use by the army. It probably was an army weapon, perhaps belonging to the same trooper who had worn the pants the brave now wore.

The carbine fired below, and Spur jumped as did most of the Indians in the camp. The brave laughed. He went through the process again, instructing another brave how to pull down and forward the trigger guard lever to eject the used round. He then showed the brave how to load in a cartridge and push the trigger guard back in position.

The teacher made his student go over the routine five times, then helped him to aim and fire. From the way the Indian demonstrated the technique of holding and firing the weapon, Spur knew he must have been an army scout or had been around army weapons training. This one Indian at least was looking for a fight. He and Chitsa watched as four different braves took their basic training with the carbine. Spur wondered how much ammunition they had.

They pulled back from the skyline of the ridge.

"You said it looks like they're moving out," said Spur.

"Yes. The squaws are packing up, loading everything. In Indian society, the women do *all* the work. The men only lie around and brag, make babies, hunt and go to war." She was laughing, then sobered. "I'd guess this camp will be broken up within an hour and they will move on to another buffalo hunt. They don't have the big tipis, the pottery. This is just a hunting camp."

They moved back to the top and watched. Six more braves went through rifle training, and now it was obvious to Spur that they had only one Sharps. There was no war paint, no dancing. The braves were getting in some instruction as the squaws got ready to move. Some of the braves worked on hunting equipment. Two older men sat chipping spear points out of large slabs of obsidian. They used a hard rock and struck the obsidian a sharp blow with a hammer-like rock which chipped a flake off the obsidian. By chipping away at the right spot, the craftsman could fashion a sturdy, sharp spear point with a flange at the end for tying to the spear end.

Two more braves worked at fastening feathers onto their arrows.

The Indian horses were kept in a rope corral farther up the ravine. Now, one by one, horses were brought up and big baskets made of buffalo hide were fitted over the mounts' sides and filled with meat, tools and camp goods.

Within an hour the camp was struck. Only the fire pit showed that anyone had been living there. The big tipi had been taken down and formed into a travois pulled by two horses. It was piled with lighter goods, freshly scraped buffalo hides, and carried one old woman who evidently couldn't walk.

When Chitsa saw it she stared in wonder.

"Who could she be?" Spur asked.

"I don't know," Chitsa said. "Strange, unusual. In most Indian societies, when the old can no longer produce and work for the good of the tribe, they are sent away. They simply walk into the desert or the mountains or the plains and when they get exhausted, they lie down and die. There is no heroics, no charity, and no compassion. This old woman must be someone important.''

"The chief's mother?"

A look of knowing scorn shaded her pretty face. "Of course not! The chief's mother would be the first to know that she was not contributing. She would build a small fire in front of her tipi or lodge, welcome all of her friends around and talk of the wonderful days when they were young. When the fire went out, the talking would stop. The old woman would get to her feet and walk away to die. Her name would never be spoken again.''

They watched the last brave mount and ride away and saw one squaw go over the camp carefully to find anything left behind. Then she, the squaws and the children walked single file behind the procession of Indian ponies as they wound into the valley and around a bend.

Chitsa jumped up and ran, following them, keeping them in sight but remaining hidden herself. Spur followed her. At a vantage point half a mile away, they watched the little band working its way slowly across the valley and toward the far slope. When the tribe was far enough away, Chitsa said they would not come back, so the two observers retraced their steps and went down to the campsite.

Spur found the spot where the men had fired the rifle and picked up two of the brass casings. They were .50 caliber. He pushed them in his pocket.

Chitsa prowled the camp. She found a knife, but the point was broken off. Under some brush she found a small buffalo skin bag and inside a good knife with a four-inch blade. She smiled and kept both.

Spur could find nothing else to help him. He went to the place where the large tipi had been. The grass was matted down where the floor of the tipi had been laid, but he found nothing of interest. He prowled the outer rim of the tipi location. Something caught his eye in the trampled down grass. Spur bent and picked it up. In his hand he held a piece of gold. It looked as if it had been melted down and cast in a round form of some kind, then hammered. The shape of a flying bird had been delicately carved into the soft squaw clay. He showed it to Chitsa.

"Squaw clay," Chitsa said. "The chief's squaw is going to be furious with herself for losing it." Chitsa turned it over in her hand. "The art work is very good."

"You know that's gold?"

"Yes. Some of the squaws in the Black Hills find gold and melt it down in a hot fire and form it in wooden molds. Then they pound it and shape it and carve it to form trinkets. The braves say the soft metal is not good for anything. They want steel for their knives and tomahawk blades."

"You know what happened in California in Forty-Nine?"

"Sutter's Mill—the gold rush. Yes. It sent millions of people rushing to California."

"You know what a gold rush would do to the Black Hills? What would happen to the miners who tried to come in here?"

"The first thousand would be slaughtered by the angry Sioux. Then the army would move in and slaughter the Sioux. But for that to happen there would have to be massive amounts of gold in the Black Hills. I don't think there is that much. The stories I've heard is that the squaw clay is hard to find, except for the *Rio del Oro.*"

"Spanish?" Spur asked, surprised. "River of gold. What's a Spanish name doing up here?"

"Some Spanish missionary came here more than a hundred years ago, that's the story I've heard. It isn't a big river and the gold stretch isn't that long. That's all I know. The story may be just somebody's creative imagination. But there *is* gold in the Black Hills."

"And the more people who hear about it, the more trouble we're going to have with the Sioux. Damn!"

"It's there, Spur. And one of these days there *will* be a gold rush. Nothing we do will stop it or slow it down. We'd better get back under cover."

They went into the woods and Spur stared again at the carved piece of gold. He hefted it in his hand. Three, maybe four ounces. It was worth over a hundred dollars! Millions of workers in the East toiled six months to make a hundred dollars. He slipped the gold into his pocket and they moved deeper into the woods.

"I'd like to see one more Indian camp. Are there any close around?"

Chitsa shook her head, her long black hair flying freely.

"Not that I saw. I could take another scouting mission."

They came to a small cleared place in the woods on their way back to their horses. Spur was still trying to decide if he had seen enough.

"*Eiiiiiiiiiiyaaaaaaaaaaaa!*"

The sudden Indian war cry lanced through the trees and into Spur's consciousness as two Indians on horses charged out of the brush twenty yards ahead of them. Both had bows and arrows and were drawing them for the kill.

"No guns!" Chitsa screeched.

Spur knew instantly what she meant. A gunshot now would bring every brave in the hunting party racing back here. Chitsa and Spur both darted behind big pine trees before the braves could loose their arrows.

Spur held the long gun. No rifle shots. What now? He would shoot as a last resort, he decided. It was obvious the Indians were charging ahead. He could hear the hooves pounding in the rocky soil. Spur took a chance and peered around the tree. Both braves were continuing their charge straight at the trees where Chitsa and Spur hid. Spur's mind raced. What in hell was he supposed to do now?

# CHAPTER THIRTEEN

In the ten seconds he had left before the two mounted Sioux braves were upon them, Spur looked at
Chitsa and saw she had drawn the big knife. She
held it in her right hand high over her head behind
the tree.

He *did* have a weapon. Spur turned the Spencer
around, holding it by the barrel, and lifted it. It
would make a deadly club.

The riders were almost upon them. His timing
would have to be perfect. No time to take a look. He
would strike when he first saw the muzzle of the
first horse coming past the tree.

The snorting flaring nostrils suddenly appeared
and Spur swung the Spencer downward. He was
slightly early—the heavy butt of the Spencer came
down just in front of the brave's head, but the forward motion of the horse slammed the Indian's
throat into the heavy wooden stock, jolting his head
backward. Spur heard a sharp crack like the breaking of a dry stick. The Sioux brave's head rolled to

one side, his eyes blank and staring, the drawn bow falling from his hand. He slid sideways on his mount, tumbled toward Spur and fell to the ground a dozen feet beyond, his arms against another pine tree and the pony running like a fleet mule deer through the woods.

The Indian didn't move. Spur looked at the tree Chitsa had hidden behind. He had heard no sound, but now Spur saw that the other Sioux brave had gotten off his horse. One hand held a long slash on his side where blood drained through his fingers. In his other hand he held a knife and advanced on Chitsa, deadly fury in his every movement.

Spur wanted to shoot the savage in the heart, but he knew he couldn't. He drew back the Spencer and shouted, running toward the brave. The Indian never looked back, concentrating on his primary target.

Spur got to the Indian from the side, and swung the Spencer. It slammed into the Indian's side, breaking his ribs and driving him to the ground on his stomach.

Before he could get up, Chitsa darted in, dove on the Sioux's back and her right hand brought the knife across the brave's throat. In one desperate move the red man turned over and Chitsa stared at the slash across his throat. Blood spurted from both arteries as the Sioux's arms dropped to his side. His eyes rolled upward and his head turned to the side.

Spur lifted Chitsa from the corpse, picked her up and hurried with her into the deeper timber. He expected to hear her start crying, but she didn't. Spur put her down next to a large pine, and sat beside her.

Chitsa stared straight ahead, eyes unblinking,

face in total repose as if she were sleeping.

"Chitsa," he said softly. "Chitsa, you did what you had to do. He was trying to kill you. He could have sent you on a journey to the hereafter right now."

She didn't move. He had seen the same thing happen in the war—the sudden shock of killing or seeing a friend die or sometimes being wounded. Spur slapped her, a sharp, stinging blow on the cheek which turned her head around.

"No!" Her voice came with sudden anger. "Don't hit me!"

Spur looked at her again and saw her eyes moving. She took a deep breath and sighed. Then a tear seeped from the corner of her eye and then another and a moment later she leaned into his arms, sobbing her heart out.

She was still crying five minutes later, and Spur lifted her and carried her toward the horses. Soon she pushed away and indicated she wanted to walk. He let her down but held firmly to her hand.

"Chitsa, you did only what you knew you must. You were right. The Sioux would have killed you like stepping on a bug."

"But. . . . but there were two of us! It was not fair!"

"It was not fair for them to attack us with arrows when we had none. Did that stop *them?*"

"No." Her response was barely loud enough to hear.

"We are alive, Chitsa, that is the most important thing. To be dead and absolutely right might be satisfying to posterity, but it certainly isn't much fun."

She didn't respond.

"Chitsa, how long before the braves will be missed?"

"What?"

"How long before those two Sioux will be missed and someone goes looking for them?"

"If they were a day hunting party, it would be several hours. If they were scouts, an hour or two. If they were on a long range hunt it might be days."

"Then we must head back, right now, as quickly as we can. Is there cover for us to move back south?"

"I think so."

"We have to know for sure. Chitsa, is there cover?"

She looked at him, her face changing from despair to a degree of hope. "Yes—I can find enough. It will be dark in three hours. We must find the horses and start now and travel all night. You must feed the horses the oats the first chance you get. They will need all of their strength. We will canter for half an hour, then walk them for an hour, and canter again." She nodded. "Yes, both are strong and deep chested, they can stand that pace for at least ten hours. Then we will be out of the greatest danger."

He lifted her up and kissed her, holding her tightly. "You are a marvel, pretty little Indian maid. Any other woman I know in this situation would have screamed, dissolved in tears and hysterics and been dead within seconds. That would have given the other brave time to sight in on me as I finished his partner, and I would be heading for Heaven myself. You are magnificent!" He kissed her again. She kissed him back, then squirmed in his strong arms.

"Quickly now, quickly! We must travel."

They found the horses where they had been tied, and rode at a gallop for the first quarter mile, slowed to a walk for ten minutes through the timber at the edges of the valley, then went over the ridge and re-traced part of their route.

It was just past midnight when Spur called a halt. He figured they had traveled almost thirty miles. The tall timber was behind them, and they were into the grasslands again. There would be little cover during the daylight, so they would have to be careful.

They ate his can of sliced peaches, and the last of the tinned beef. Then they pushed on for four more hours before they found a good hiding spot for the day.

Chitsa was so tired she could barely sit her saddle. He helped her dismount, spread the blankets for her and watched while she fell into a deep sleep at once.

Spur pondered their trip. So far he had discovered enough to make it worth while. There was no way he could determine who among the redmen was contacting the Camp. A 24-hour watch on the post might turn up someone leaving to make contact with a renegade, but even that might not be productive.

Twice that night Chitsa woke up screaming. Spur held her, quieted her, talked gently to her until the fear vanished and she slept soundly once more.

It was almost eight in the morning when Spur awoke. They had planned on staying there for the rest of the day, but something urged Spur to change the decision.

Chitsa had not awakened yet. At ten that morning he kissed her eyes and then her lips and her arms came around him. She sat up quickly, saw him and smiled. Then she shivered.

"I had the most terrible dreams. It was awful. Why didn't you wake me sooner?"

"You needed the sleep. The dreams will pass. You'll gradually forget about it."

"No, never! I killed a human being—another Indian!"

"He was also trying to kill you."

"Yes, that's what I keep telling myself, but it doesn't help much." She stood up, then walked to the front of the wooded area and studied the plains.

When she came back she nodded. "You want to move on, right?"

He said he did.

"We're well out of the Black Hills now. Our chances of running into any Sioux are very slim." They built a fire, made coffee and, after finishing the last of the second cup, mounted up and rode.

They covered nearly fifty miles that day, fed the horses oats and settled down for a good sleep.

Chitsa rolled over toward him. "When we get back to the Camp it will be impossible for us to be together. Could you love me once more?"

They made love twice softly, with much tenderness, then went to sleep in each other's arms.

Late the next night they reached Camp Sheridan. As they had arranged, Spur went in alone. She would stay in the woods along the river for two more days, then come back alone.

Spur let a trooper take care of his horse and reported directly to the commanding officer's quarters. Colonel Underhill had been reading a book and slammed it shut when Spur came in.

149

"Thunder, man! Couldn't it wait until morning? It's almost ten o'clock!"

"And I could be coming in to tell you five-thousand Sioux are on the warpath. Would that be important?"

Col. Underhill looked up, his eyes alive. "The bastards are finally going to turn and fight, are they?"

"No, Colonel, the Sioux are *not* on the warpath. But they *are* learning how to use the rifles they have been getting. I watched for half an hour as one brave wearing cavalry pants taught every other brave in his camp how to load and fire a Sharps carbine."

"I hope you shot the bastard where he stood!"

"If I had, Colonel, I wouldn't have made it back alive to tell you this. My report will show that the Sioux are hunting right now, laying in their winter's food supply. They continue to object strongly to any whites invading their home territory. And it is my determination that they are preparing their braves to use the rifles they hope to get soon."

"So we must take four hundred men and go through the hills and kill every Indian we can find!" Col. Underhill said, his eyes flashing, his breath coming fast. "We can have two hundred men ready in six hours. We'll move out at noon tomorrow!"

"Colonel, you don't have any orders authorizing you to undertake any such campaign. That has to come straight from headquarters."

"Hell, we'll do it anyway! An officer's got to use some initiative to get along in this man's army."

"You go in there, and I'll have you courtmartialed."

*"Bastard!"*

"Colonel, have you thought of retiring? I don't think you're in good enough health to command this camp."

Colonel Underhill began laughing. He slapped his sides and roared for two minutes, then he was on his feet and his .44 revolver was pointed at Spur's chest.

"Soldier, you say anything like that again, and I'll shoot you dead where you sit! No brag. I'll kill you! I'm the best damn commander in Nebraska, Omaha included. Told them that. Told Phil Sheridan that. What the fuck does he know? Damn skirt chaser, regular cock hound, the son-of-a-bitch!"

Spur started to stand.

"Don't move, Colonel! Hate to have to shoot you down with you in the prime of life. Got to get my damned birds. My eagles. Got to! Damn brother-in-law got his last year. He'll make general if the bastard lives long enough." Colonel Underhill sat down, waving the six-gun at the ceiling.

Spur decided a sudden change of subject might bring the colonel out of his sudden disorientation.

"Colonel, did I tell you about the herd of buffalo I saw? One bunch was as near as across the parade grounds. Two or three huge bulls, a few cows and some calves as frisky as puppies."

"Buffalo?" Colonel Underhill turned and looked at Spur. "Aren't many buffalo around the camp here."

"No sir. I was up toward the Black Hills. Lots of them up there. But I never ran into a large herd."

The colonel looked at Spur, suddenly interested. "Yes—your trip into the Black Hills. I warned you it would be dangerous. Tell me, Colonel, just how did it go?"

Spur went through what he had said before. "So, Colonel, I think we should keep an extra tight inventory control on all rifles and carbines on the post, and make sure every man has only the weapon he signed out for."

"Yes, yes, fine idea, Colonel McCoy. I'll get a sergeant on that first thing tomorrow. If you think there's anything else we should do, you be sure to let me know." He saw the pistol in his hand, broke it open and Spur saw it was unloaded. He sighted through the bore. "I was about to clean this. Should keep a side arm as clean and well-oiled as possible."

Spur agreed, and after a few more words, took his leave. He was still worried about the colonel, but there was nothing he could do, not yet.

# CHAPTER FOURTEEN

Buffalo Kane was waiting for Spur when he left the commander's office. The scout fell into step beside Spur and grinned foolishly in the soft light of the half moon.

"Evening. Heard you was back. Got a minute?"

Spur knew Kane had been drinking, but the man did have a problem.

"Sure, Kane." Spur looked at him expectantly.

Kane motioned toward the two chairs sitting outside the sutler's store. They sat down and Kane leaned forward.

"Remember I told you I was hunting the killers of my family? Well, I think I found them—at least one of the bastards. Sort of like you to come with me and see what you think."

"I assume you're going through the proper army channels."

Kane laughed. "Damn right I am! Hail, colonel, I'm still under contract with the fucking army. Another twenty days. I got to go through channels or I get my butt reamed out, right?"

"Quite true, Kane."

"Well, why don't we wander down there then, and I'll let you give me your sayso."

"Where?"

"Down by the back gate."

"Seems like a strange place for a courtmartial."

"Well, we ain't quite at that stage yet. Just got some evidence I want you to take a quick gander at."

"Fine, let's go. It's been a long day for me."

They walked past the barracks to the stables. Behind the stables, Kane drew his .44 and held it on Spur.

"Now, Colonel, just keep walking. We go out the back gate and down to the river. Most nigh a quarter of a mile but I'd bet my ass you can walk that far even without an army mule under your bottom."

"Kane, you don't need the weapon. You want me to go down there, I'll go."

"Right, Colonel. Right. And you're a fucking bird colonel and I'm a lousy almost-run-out-of-the-army scout all 'cause I had an Indian family. Yeah. Now let's go. I'll kinda have my old .44 down beside my leg here, Colonel, so we don't 'tract no attention, but she's there and she's ready to shoot. Let's walk."

They went out the gate, past the guard who merely waved at Kane and paid no attention to Spur.

It was a short walk and they soon came to the water, turned left downstream for a hundred feet to a big elm tree.

Spur saw the rope looped over a large branch and hanging down. It cut a path across the moon. When Spur followed it down, he found a man standing on a

154

wooden box. The man's hands were tied behind him, and the rope was fastened around his neck. Spur was not surprised to see an authentic hangman's knot tied around the man's throat.

"Kane, if this is some kind of a joke . . ."

"Ask *him*, Colonel. It sure as shit ain't no joke! Go on, ask him. That's the son-of-a-bitch who murdered my wife and my two sons!"

"Kane, listen to reason a moment," the man on the box said. Spur recognized the voice. It was Lt. Casselberry.

"Shut up, you killer!" Kane shouted. "You'll get your chance to defend yourself. We got us a judge and jury now. Colonel McCoy wil listen to the evidence, give the verdict and then I'll kick that box out from under you and watch you hang! Only you got to know *why*. The *why* is because you killed my family!"

Kane's voice soared upward at the end until he was screaming.

Spur walked up to Casselberry.

"Lieutenant, have you entered a plea to the court?"

"Yes, sir. Not guilty."

"Thank you. Mr. Prosecutor, you may begin. What evidence do you have to support your charges?"

"A lot, your honor. I come home on the afternoon of April 2, 1870, from a patrol and found my wife, Walking Fawn, and my two sons killed by regulation army rounds. The brass was all over the place. The bastards didn't give them a chance!"

"Mr. Kane, no opinion allowed. Just state the facts."

"Yeah. My wife had a gold medallion—I found the gold myself and pounded it into a circle and fixed it up. She loved it. It was stole and turned up later at the sutler's store. Two troopers turned it in for some beer. It was my wife's. I bought it back. The troopers said Lt. Casselberry sold it to them for ten dollars."

"Mr. Kane, are you prepared to bring those two troopers to this court to testify?"

"Your honor—Colonel—one of them deserted last week, and the other was killed about three weeks ago on a patrol. They can't testify."

"What other evidence do you have, Mr. Kane?"

"There was just one set of horseshoe prints around my place that day. Just one bastard rode in to loot the cabin and look at the bodies. One horseshoe had the tip broken off on the left front hoof, same as the horse that Lt. Casselberry still rides. He done it, plain as the sunshine in the morning."

"Is that your evidence, Mr. Kane?"

"Shitpot full should be enough, your honor!"

"Thank you, Mr. Kane. Now for the defense. I assume you will be representing yourself, Lt. Casselberry."

"Yes, damnit! Can we get this charade over with? Colonel, I have never seen that gold piece before. I did not sell anything even resembling it to any enlisted man. If I had the gold I would have kept it and exchanged it for its true value of something over a hundred dollars. Secondly, yes, my horse had a broken shoe. I noticed it just this morning and had it changed today. Mr. Kane happened to see the farrier at work, which gave him his idea for these trumped-up charges."

"Your testimony is taken under consideration, Lieutenant. Is there anything else?"

"Yes, Colonel. The raid on the Kane family was made the afternoon of April 1, as close as our people could tell. We investigated, but could come to no conclusions other than that it appeared that some army unit or army personnel had indeed gunned down Mr. Kane's family. On that day, April 1, I was on patrol with twenty men of B company. We were searching for a missing Conestoga wagon and a party of four civilians. We found them, all deceased and the wagon burned. We returned the afternoon of April 2, arriving at camp at about three o'clock. The scout on our patrol was Buffalo Kane."

Spur turned toward where the scout had been standing, but he was no longer there. He spoke into the darkness. "Mr. Kane, we have some contradictory testimony here. Would you tell the court for the record, who the officers were on the patrol you were on which ended April 2?"

"No!" a voice said from behind Spur. "There sure as hell wasn't no bastard called Casselberry on it, that's for damn sure. Check with Major Rutherford. He's got the records." Kane's voice went high and wild again.

"Mr. Kane, are you ready for the court's decision?"

"Hell yes, and I'm ready to kick that box out!"

"Mr. Kane, I've heard all the evidence, examined what is reasonable and practical. I have weighed the contradictory evidence and have come to my decision. Are you prepared to accept the verdict of this court?"

"Yeah, yeah, get on with it."

"I, Colonel Spur McCoy, United States Army, presiding at this special courtmartial, do find and declare the accused, one Lt. Neil Casselberry, innocent of the charge of killing . . ."

Spur never got the sentence finished. Buffalo Kane burst out of the darkness, dove at the wooden box holding Lt. Casselberry and slammed into it with his shoulder.

Spur dug out his .44 to go for Kane, but he was too late. He saw the box tilt and start to slant outward. He could see the slack tightening in the rope over the tree limb; he knew the fall would be enough to snap Lt. Casselberry's neck. Spur was too far away to catch him. His .44 came up and he fired, pointing his weapon at the rope over the limb. Four times he shot, faster than he ever had before, and the second round caught the rope in the center, snapping two of the three strands.

When the box toppled, an immediate strain went on the rope and the remaining strand was not enough to take the increasing weight of Lt. Casselberry's body. When he came to the end of the stretch, the last strand over the limb broke and Neil Casselberry hit the riverbank on his feet and tumbled to his knees. The hangman's noose did not break the officer's neck. All it did was put a minor rope burn around his throat.

Spur got to Casselberry quickly, cut the ropes off his wrists and lifted the noose away from his neck.

For a moment Lt. Casselberry couldn't speak. He had come within one .44 slug of meeting his maker and he knew it. He stared at Spur, then at the frayed end of the rope. Then looked down at Buffalo Kane and realized that the scout had passed out.

"Are you all right, Casselberry?" Spur asked.

"Yes, sir. But I got the shit scared out of me. Jesus!"

"He had himself convinced you were the guilty man," Spur said. "I'm glad I got back when I did."

"He would have waited. I've been standing on that box for two hours, and he's been drinking for two days. He'll sleep it off. When he gets sober he won't remember a thing about any of this."

"There was an official investigation about Kane's family?"

"Yes. Shall we go back? My wife will be worried."

They turned walking toward camp.

"Major Rutherford was incensed by the killings. Underhill thought it was a joke. The major called in every officer who wasn't on my patrol and questioned him. He thought he had it narrowed down to three men, but when he called the troopers to testify with total immunity, not a man came in."

"Did Rutherford hit it too hard?"

"That was the talk around the officers' side. The E.M. were afraid they would get burned right along with the officers, even though they had no choice but to follow the officer's orders."

"Who were the three men the major narrowed it down to?"

"He wouldn't say."

"The guilty man had to have been on some kind of patrol or training outside the camp that day."

"All three were. I narrowed it down myself. It had to be either Lt. Wes Pauley, Lt. Omer Imhoff or a man who transferred out a week ago, Lt. Dabler. He was a patsy, a by-the-book soldier. He wasn't cut out for murder."

"Does Buffalo Kane know this?"

"He will tomorrow. When he sobers up and gets rid of his hangover I'm going to tell him. What he *doesn't* know almost got me hanged."

They walked to the stables.

"If you had to pick one of the two suspects, which one would you choose?"

"Imhoff every time. But then I don't like the son-of-a-bitch, so my vote doesn't count." The young officer hesitated. "Colonel, I know I said some things I shouldn't have when we first talked. I was almost out of my head with worry. Things have been easing off a bit here now—about my wife."

Spur nodded. "Good. I'm glad to hear it. The army needs conscientious and honest young officers."

"Thank you, sir. I . . . What happened tonight was so unbelievable that I can hardly conceive of it. This fantasy with Buffalo Kane—I'm embarrassed about how he caught me. He said he had something to show me down by the stables I'd be interested in, and once we got there he pulled his pistol and marched me out the gate and down to the tree. He was wild drunk then, and I figured he'd just as soon shoot me as hang me. Hanging sounded slower. I talked him into a trial with you as the judge. He had the rope and the box and everything ready. I didn't get scared until he put me on that damn wobbly box and tied off the rope tight.

"Colonel, that hour alone down there in the dark is about as scared as I ever want to get. What I'm saying is, you saved my life tonight. I don't know how one man thanks another for something like that. But anyway, thanks for my life. I appreciate it."

"Casselberry, that's what colonels are made for.

160

Just see that Buffalo Kane knows about his choice being down to two. He only has three weeks left.''

Lt. Neil Casselberry said he'd take care of it in the morning, snapped a West Point perfect salute which Spur returned, and the young officer walked off toward his quarters.

Spur watched him go for a moment, then turned toward his own room. He had not felt so sore, tired and washed out in a long time. The idea that he might have to make the ride back into the Black Hills soon was not exciting.

He found his room all cleaned and ready for him. There was fresh fruit in a bowl on the dresser and clean sheets on the bed. He imagined Molly had fixed it all for him. Right then he wanted nothing more than to test out the sheets. But he did wonder how long the army would continue the "laundress" system. Someone in his superior understanding had decreed that each army camp and installation would have one laundress for each nineteen-and-a-half enlisted men. The women who did the laundry were usually the wives of enlisted men, though the army actually discouraged the marriage of the troopers. Any enlisted man who wanted to get married had to get permission from his commanding officer. If there were too many laundresses on a post, the permission was denied.

Spur forgot about Molly, forgot about gold and forgot about missing army rifles. He barred the front door, put a solid chair under the back one and locked it, then undressed and slid into bed and immediately fell asleep.

# CHAPTER FIFTEEN

The same night Spur arrived at Camp Sheridan, a tired, still slightly awed Indian girl changed her mind about propriety and slipped into the camp and into her room in the Underhill quarters through her open window, as she always did after her outings.

She brushed her long hair, braided it carefully in one long plait falling down her back, and went to bed. She tried to figure which day it was. Each day there was some social function for the officers' wives. Tomorrow was Monday or Tuesday. Or was it Wednesday? She would have to put in an appearance, no matter what day it was. For just a moment she thought about the man she had killed. She would never forget the look in his eyes as he died. She wondered if she would sleep.

She did, dropping off at once. She did not have any bad dreams.

The next morning Chitsa helped Grace Underhill prepare breakfast as usual. Chitsa said she'd had a wonderful time in the open, watching the animals sleeping under the night sky, living as she had as a child. Grace had made a habit of not prying, but she did wonder. She made absolutely no connection between the time Chitsa was gone and Colonel McCoy's absence. She wasn't even aware that Spur was back in camp.

The women's meeting that day was in the Colonel's parlor, and the ladies would gather for tatting, embroidery, point lace, crocheting and knitting. There was usually one of the women who could instruct them all in one of the types of needlework.

Janet Casselberry came in precisely on time, ten o'clock. She didn't want to come too late or too early. It was the first of the social affairs she had attended since her return. She wore her prettiest dress, and her long blonde hair was freshly washed and knotted demurely at the back of her head. She smiled so hard her cheeks hurt, and took Grace Underhill's hand.

"Grace, I just had to come today. I'm feeling fine, none the worse for wear. I was scared spitless out there in the wilds, but it turned out fine after all. That nice Colonel McCoy came along and like a perfect gentleman brought me straight back to camp. I know I'm the luckiest person in the world not to have met any Indians. I must have been born under a lucky star!"

Grace Underhill beamed. She was so glad to see Janet, and to see her looking so well. Obviously the rumors she'd heard were all nonsense. She beamed and put Janet beside her for the tatting lesson they would have that day. Six more women arrived promptly. Two of them sniffed and moved away from Janet, but the others smiled and said hello and treated her much as usual.

Chitsa came in quietly and sat to one side, her nimble fingers flying as she worked on tatting some squares for an armchair. Some of the women nodded, the rest ignored her. She was, after all, only an Indian.

When all the ladies were assembled, nine today, Janet cleared her throat and they all looked at her expectantly.

"Ladies, I haven't seen you for several days. I've been resting. I had quite an experience, and I'll certainly *never* get lost again. I simply turned the wrong way and before I realized it, the night had closed in and I was totally turned around. I found some trees and I sat up most of the night, but at last I nodded off toward sunrise. Then I got my bearings and began walking, but somehow I became confused by the trees and the river and I went the wrong way again.

"But with my lucky star watching over me, I did not meet up with any of the Sioux hunting parties that sometimes come close to camp. Then Colonel McCoy found me and gave me a ride back to camp. He was a perfect gentleman, naturally, and I'm ever so thankful he did find me."

A pale young woman in her twenties sniffed. "That is unusual, Janet, dear. My Willy says there always are a few Sioux hunters upstream on the White. Says it would be an absolute *miracle* if any woman could be out there two whole days and not be caught by some Sioux hunting party."

"Willy wasn't there, Mrs. Crowder," Janet said sweetly.

Sitting beside Mrs. Crowder was Milicent Orlando. She was known as the camp's biggest gossip, and was always willing to invent a few embellishments as she passed on a tale.

"Janet, dear, we all are just terrified of something like that happening to us. And you know we *are* curious. I can't think of anything worse than to have an Indian capture me. Just *thinking* about it must have been awful! I mean, those savages—to have them touch me, and tear at my clothes, then to throw me down in the grass and . . . well, you know. I just don't . . . "

"Stop it!" a voice shouted. Everyone looked up at the sound and found Chitsa glaring at them. "The two of you should be thrown out of this house and horsewhipped! You are cruel and insulting! You are snide, insinuating and gossips and tellers of tall tales. I don't like either one of you!

"If this were my house, neither Mrs. Crowder or Mrs. Orlando would be invited back. If Janet says she became lost and was found by the colonel, I believe her. Most everyone in this camp does! If it weren't for a pair of tattling busybodies with nothing better to do than make up stories, the whole thing would have been forgotten days ago!" Chitsa ran and knelt in front of Grace Underhill. "I apologize if I have embarrassed you in your own house. I will go. I'm not sure I can live with whites anymore. I never could if they were all like those two." She rose, moved over to Janet, bent down and kissed both her cheeks. Janet reached out and hugged her. Then Chitsa marched out the front door and walked toward the river.

In the room Chitsa had just left, the ladies sat in shocked silence. Never before had Chitsa said a half dozen words at their socials. She had been there watching with her black eyes, absorbing every word.

Grace Underhill took a deep breath. "Ladies, Chitsa as you just heard, has strong opinions and a definite mind of her own. She is a guest in my house, as are all of you, but I do apologize if she has hurt anyone's feelings. We are a small society here. We must strive to be friends and to get along with each other.

"Chitsa is a sensitive person, shy and quiet. She is Indian, a Shawnee from southern Ohio. She was naturally upset about all that talk about bad Indians. She's been with us for almost fifteen years, but sometimes I don't really know her. She spends a lot of time with her books."

"She's beautiful," one of the ladies said. "What I wouldn't give to have long luxurious hair like that!"

There were some murmurs of approval.

Janet Casselberry sat in a soft glow. She didn't dare to look at anyone, but she was sure it was over. Now there would be no more gossip about her, no stories. Neil could relax.

"You say Chitsa reads a lot?" another woman said. "Goodness, she sounds so *educated.* She sounds like one of those college educated girls. I am impressed."

Two more of the ladies remarked about Chitsa's intelligence, her evident book learning.

Then Mrs. Grove, the instructor of tatting, got them busy on their work.

The session was over early so the ladies could get home and fix their men's noon meal. Janet bustled around her small kitchen, humming, slicing bread baked fresh that morning, knowing it was all over, realizing that one small Indian girl had waded in where she could not go and had slain the giant!

She was humming when Neil came in after his drill. He was tired and dusty. She brought a pan of cool water and washed off his face and arms. Then she told him about Chitsa.

"She was just magnificent! She stood up to those biddies as I could never do."

Lt. Casselberry smiled. "The women will tell their husbands and that should end the whole thing." He reached over and kissed her. "Hey, pretty girl. Would you mind if we skipped the food and I nibbled on you instead?"

"I was hoping you would say that!" She unbuttoned his shirt and kissed her way down his hard, muscled stomach.

Casselberry groaned with desire. "Keep right on kissing," he murmured. She looked up, kissed his lips and forced her tongue into his mouth, pressing her body eagerly against his.

"Darling, that sounds like such a delightful idea. I'll kiss you all over, and then you can nibble me to pieces!"

He lifted his brows. "I never knew you wanted me to—that you would let me."

He led her to the bedroom then, and they enjoyed each other so much Lt. Casselberry was a half hour late getting back to his troop for its weekly inspection. He didn't mind the delay in the least. His men wondered what had happened. It was the easiest and most casual inspection they had undergone in months.

# CHAPTER SIXTEEN

That same morning Spur McCoy sat in Major Rutherford's office talking about the murder of the Kane family.

"I swear to you, McCoy, there would be nothing I'd like more than to find that officer and see him shot. Whichever man it was knew damn well that those people were protected. All my suspects had been in camp long enough to know that. It was simply blood lust."

"And there's nothing you can do now?"

"Not without some evidence. We think our officer corps is a tight little unit. Hell, we can't hold a torch to those enlisted men. There must be forty, maybe sixty men out there who know *exactly* what happened that day. But their code won't let them talk. I must have come down too hard on the whole thing. No one will come forward now."

A sergeant came into the room.

"Sir, you said to let you know about the patrol. It will be formed up at noon. The twenty men have eaten and will be ready for the four day march. The normal supply train should be met about halfway here, south of Box Butte somewhere. The supplies will be off loaded from the train at Sidney, and put on our re-supply wagons which are already at the station."

"Very good, Sergeant. Lt. Imhoff has volunteered for the mission. He'll be leading it. Our scout is ill and can't make the trip. Issue a hundred and forty rounds per man. There shouldn't be any trouble riding due south."

The sergeant saluted and left the room.

"Regular re-supply?" Spur asked.

Major Rutherford nodded, looked away and stood up. "Dammit, I guess I can tell you. There also is a shipment of fifty new rifles on this load. With the trouble we've been having about missing rifles, I'm a little edgy."

If the local rifle smuggler knew about this shipment, it would be an ideal time to steal more weapons for the Indians. Only how do you fight off a twenty-man patrol? Kill them all? Not likely. It would make more sense to meet the wagons a day and a half out. It was at least a three day ride. Spur had just done it. He made up his mind in a hurry.

"Sir, I'd like to ride along with that escort."

"Why, Colonel?"

"Rifles, fifty of them. That's a big prize for some rampaging Sioux. And then Imhoff is leading it. Isn't he one of your prime suspects in the Kane massacre?"

"Who told you that?"

"A friend. Did you know that Buffalo Kane almost hanged Lt. Casselberry last night?"

"I heard. Thanks for your help." The major thought for a minute. "You really want to go on this supply run?"

"Yes."

"Fine. I couldn't stop you if I wanted to, but I don't want to. Watch yourself. I have a bad feeling about this."

An hour later Spur was at the head of the cavalry column beside Lt. Imhoff. Major Rutherford had given the young officer instructions; if they ran into any kind of action, or were attacked, Colonel McCoy was the commanding officer. Imhoff shrugged, nodded and they moved out.

A few wives came to the rear gate to see them off, then the double column stretched out over the prairie as they moved at a lope toward the south. Spur couldn't decide why he had chosen to come on the patrol. A hunch, he supposed as the miles melted away beneath the horses' hooves. A strong hunch that something was going to go wrong. Nothing he could pin down. He'd been following hunches all his life.

The second day at dusk, they hadn't met the wagons. Imhoff sent out scouts to watch for dust just before dark, but they came back and reported seeing no sign of the dust trail or any movement for at least ten miles ahead.

Imhoff didn't seem worried. "Hell, they could have missed the course, gone up another valley. Might have had a late start. They can't make more than twelve, fifteen miles a day with those heavy wagons. They started five days ago. That should put them somewhere about halfway. But who knows? They might have lost some time with broken axles, anything. This ain't exactly the Washington D.C. turnpike they got to travel down here."

Spur nodded. He didn't like it, but there wasn't much he could do. The logic was sound. But there seemed to be something else there, some undercurrent. Then he had it. The superior grin that touched Imhoff's lips now and then. Was it only when he thought he wasn't being watched?

As he lay on his blanket that night, Spur did some figuring. Five days traveling at twelve miles a day would be sixty miles. If the escort had come out a day and a half at forty miles a day, that was also sixty miles. The whole trip should be one hundred twenty miles. Something was wrong. Spur slid out of his blankets at midnight, took his Spencer repeating rifle and his rounds of ammunition and packed up his horse. He told the guard he would be gone for a while on a scouting mission and rode to the highest promontory he could find.

Two miles away from the sleeping camp he came to a knoll and stared south. He could see no fires, no lights, no sign of white man nor Indian. He stared to the west with the same result. A sound came to him faintly, but then faded. It came again and Spur turned to hear it better.

Rifle shots!

He listened again to be sure. There was no mistaking the sound. It came from the east, at least five miles away.

Spur rode down the slope and across the prairie as fast as was safe. A canter devoured the miles, chewing them up and spitting them behind him. It took him over half an hour to cover what he guessed was five miles, where he found another small ridge and rode to the top of it. Now he could hear the rifle fire clearly. It came in single rounds, then two or three, but not a sustained fight.

Spur turned again to catch the direction. More easterly. He rode until he could hear the rifle shots over the creak of his saddle and the rushing wind of his ride. Another slight rise showed ahead. He rode up it and looked below.

A siege.

Even though most Indians didn't usually fight at night, there was some kind of attack going on below.

He spotted more than a dozen fires burning in a rough circle outside a ring of six covered army wagons. The horses were inside the circle. Evidently the commander had used the fires to keep the Indians from sneaking up in the darkness and over-running his defenses.

The whole tableau was five hundred yards away. Spur checked the surrounding area but could find no Indian campfires. They were either on the line or resting, perhaps keeping a dozen men around the wagons to keep the defenders awake and on the alert.

Spur began moving down the slope. He would go two hundred yards, leave his horse and pick out a defensive position where he could also give support to the surrounded troopers below. There was little he could do until daylight. At sunup the Sioux would probably make their attack. It was a wonder the wagons had not been captured already. Evidently there were some good soldiers down there who had a little luck on their side.

As he waited for dawn, Spur prepared his firing

position. He moved two rocks on top of the boulder he crouched behind. The slabs gave him a good firing slot and added protection. From his view of the blackness below, there seemed to be more cover on this side, so the majority of the hostiles should be below him, with their backs exposed.

Spur speculated on how the two army units could have missed one another so far. Either the supply wagons were much too far east or the escort was too far west—perhaps a little of each. But as Spur thought about it he remembered wondering two or three times where some of the landmarks were he had seen on the ride up to the fort. Maybe Lt. Imhoff had deliberately taken them by a route designed to miss the wagon train.

Spur dozed, but the first double rifle shot he had heard in some time drifted up to him and he was awake. Dawn was creeping over the eastern horizon. Spur studied the landscape below.

He could see more than a dozen bronzed bodies below behind rocks and trees, looking at the wagons. Now he could make out blue clad men under the wagons, behind boxes and a makeshift wall.

Time to go to work, Spur told himself and sighted in on the closest warrior. He triggered the round, saw the Indian below jolt with the force of the bullet and then lie still. He levered the trigger guard down, slamming another round into the Spencer and moved his aim to his next target and fired again. He killed or badly wounded five Sioux warriors before they found the blue smoke of his powder and returned fire. He heard a cheer from the wagon train, and renewed firing from the men there.

Below he could hear an Indian yelling in the quiet

of dawn, then the shapes were up and moving forward in an all-out assault. More than a dozen rifles pinned down the soldiers as their comrades ran forward. It was a surprising show of military discipline not often seen among Indian fighters. The rifles below crashed and Spur began picking off the Indians in the lead. He soon was firing single shots, not wanting to take time to load another tube. The first of the Indians had thrown flaming torches on two of the wagons, and the fighting became hand-to-hand at that point. Spur aimed his weapon at another section where the Indians had not yet reached the wagons and sent two more into their own private happy hunting ground. Spur saw the Indians concentrating on one wagon. They killed three soldiers defending it, and began rolling it away from the others, using a slight downgrade. Spur shot one man holding up the tongue, but the wagon kept rolling. As it cleared the circle of immediate fighting, the Indians swept away with it, pushing it, guiding it dians swept away with it, pushing it, guiding it down the slope until it stopped some five hundred yards below. The soldiers around the other wagons ceased firing.

The Indians brought up horses and pulled the wagon away, sending a final volley of shots at the soldiers.

Spur fired a dozen times at the Indians, hitting two at the increased range, then watched as they hitched the wagon to the Indian ponies and towed it away. Spur was about to stand up and shout to the soldiers below when a rifle round struck his rock. He bent low again.

He sensed rather than saw the figure as it hurtled over the side of his makeshift fort, a gleaming knife

174

in hand. Spur had no time to aim the Spencer. He reversed it in a vicious butt stroke. The metal base plate on the stock caught the Sioux brave under the chin and drove inward, crushing his windpipe, bursting the jugular vein and slamming him over the rock. As he fell, Spur reversed his rifle and shot the warrior in the head, exploding one eye and driving lead through his brain.

Someone shouted something from below. He listened.

"One more!" The words came through faintly. Spur slid down behind the rock and waited, his ears alert, every muscle tensed. A rock scraped to his left. Spur swung the rifle that way, jolted upward to look, then dropped back down. He had seen a brown leg extending from a rock six feet away. Spur worked the Spencer lever and loaded another round by feel, watching the top of his rock. He lifted up again quickly, the Spencer ready. The Indian had picked that exact time to take a look. Spur fired by reflex, aimed by dead reckoning, and the big Spencer blew off the top of the Indian's head.

There was a short cheer from below. Spur looked over the rock.

"Any more?" Spur bellowed toward the wagons.

"No more," came the reply.

Spur stood cautiously, ran back to where he had left his horse and rode down to the wounded supply train.

A sergeant came to meet him, snapped a salute and then grimaced. His left arm was in a sling.

"Sergeant Edwards reporting, sir."

"Edwards, looks like you were caught. How many casualties?"

"Six dead, sir, including Lieutenant Wilson. Four wounded, including Captain Robert Casemore, a replacement line officer."

"They got the wagon with the rifles in it?"

"Yes sir, and half the ammunition, almost twenty thousand rounds. How did they know we were coming?"

"I don't know, Sergeant. Your escort missed you by about ten miles. The Sioux won't be back, they got what they came for. See what you can do about making the wounded comfortable and cleaning up here. I'll go bring the escort and get you back on the road."

"Thank you, sir. If you hadn't come, they would have killed every man here."

"Never any fun to have somebody punch holes in your backside. I'll be back, Sergeant."

Spur turned and rode up the hill. He had an idea that Imhoff would hold the escort exactly where it was until Spur got back. He was right. Spur quickly ordered the men to break camp and mount up.

"You found the supply train, sir? Some of our men said they heard shots to the east."

"Some of your men were right. Sioux attacked the supply train. It got badly cut up. Let's ride."

They made it to the supply wagons in twenty minutes, and Spur put a detail to work digging graves. He took the dead soldiers' personal effects, made sure that the six remaining wagons were fit for the trail, then had a squad cut two dead horses from the traces and pull them to one side. Two of the largest mounts were drafted to go into the harness. They complained but at last settled down. An hour after the escort arrived, the six remaining wagons were on the move. One had the canvas burned off it, and a second was loaded with wounded. They rounded up the horses and had two spares which were tied to the last wagon. Spur put outriders on both sides, a three-man advance unit on the point and six men to the rear. The other troopers rode on each side of the wagons. At twelve miles a day, it would take them five days to get back to Camp Sheridan.

The wounded needed medical attention and Spur pushed the drivers so they made the trip in exactly five days. One of the wounded men died on the trip. The other three survived and Doc Jones patched them up.

Shortly after they arrived, Spur and Lt. Imhoff sat in Major Rutherford's office answering questions. The toughest one was why Imhoff had missed meeting the supply wagon.

"You should have had riders out forming a connecting link with the wagons from the first day. Why didn't you?" barked the major.

"The colonel didn't tell me to," Imhoff said.

"The colonel wasn't in charge of the escort, Imhoff, as you know. That was *your* responsibility."

"I didn't expect trouble. I planned on sending out scouts the last half of the second day. They went the wrong way."

"We also were eight miles west of the normal trail, Major." Spur said. "I just came up it last week."

"Is that true, Imhoff?"

"Not according to my reckoning, sir."

"Make out your report, Imhoff. I expect Colonel Underhill will want to have a long talk with you when he gets back."

"Where is he?" Spur asked.

"I'll tell you about that in a minute, Colonel. Any questions, Imhoff?"

"No, sir. I'll write the report."

The lieutenant did not salute as he left. He looked worried and Spur wondered why. His case would hold up—Spur had nothing on him but suspicion. When he closed the door, Major Rutherford frowned.

"We've been sending escorts to that train station for the three years I've been here. Nobody ever missed matching up before. Why this time, just when the Sioux were raiding the wagons? And how did the Indians know which wagon had the rifles in it?"

"Same questions I've been asking myself," Spur said. "Where is Colonel Underhill?"

"That may be a problem. This morning with no warning he came into my office spouting one garbled story after another. He was working himself up to something and I didn't know what. Then he showed me a set of orders. I didn't see the date on them at first. The last replacement we had brought them from Omaha about a month ago. Underhill was reading between and around the lines. The orders said something about *after* being attacked, and *when* attacked, and *if* attacked, the command held the responsibility for the protection of its own men, and the lives and property of all civilians within its zone of control. I thought I'd let him spout off and when he left, I relaxed.

"Then a half hour later I heard the bugle and he was at the head of a column of forty men, ready to ride. He told me I was in temporary command of the post and that he would come back when he had 'killed a hundred of those savages, those scum, those lice on the body of humankind, those Indians!' He rode off.''

A knock sounded on the door and the sergeant looked in.

"He's here, sir.''

"Sober?'' asked the major.

"Nearly.''

"Send him in.''

The door opened fully and Buffalo Kane walked in, blinking at the light.

"Kane, are you sober?''

"Another five minutes of walking around and I will be. If you say I got to.''

"I do.'' Rutherford frowned and shook his head. "I've heard you used to be a good tracker.''

"Hail, Major I can still track! I can follow a cougar across a sheet of rock, I can trail a Chiricahua right into his water hole.''

"Good. Can you follow a crazy colonel and forty troopers?''

"Drunk or sober, I can do that.''

"Good. We leave in half an hour. Get your gear ready.''

"Yes, sir, Major, sir.''

When Kane left, Major Rutherford looked at Spur. "Colonel Underhill told me when he left six hours ago that he was going to ride until he found some fucking Indians and kill as many as he could. He said he was behind on his 'quota,' whatever the hell he thinks that means. You want to come along, or mind the fort until I get back?''

"Captain Jones can command. I want to change clothes and get some coffee and I'll be ready. Any idea which way he rode?''

"Straight into Sioux country, heading for the Black Hills."

"I hope we can catch him in time," Spur said.

# CHAPTER SEVENTEEN

As the company of one hundred fifty men rode away from Camp Sheridan, it was four in the afternoon. They would have nearly four hours of light left. There would be little chance of tracking the troop in the dark, so they pushed their mounts into a canter and walk schedule that allowed them to move at an average of five miles an hour.

Spur knew why Major Rutherford had waited until he came back before going after his superior. To deny him his request for the troop would have been insubordination, and to counter that, Major Rutherford would have had to relieve his superior of his command. Such an extreme move could ruin two careers faster than a general courtmartial. Rutherford must not have been absolutely certain he could prove that the lives of forty men were at stake as a result of the rash and unwarranted move by the colonel.

But with Colonel McCoy along, Spur's superior rank could prevent the lieutenant colonel from continuing his charge, or doing anything else. Spur wished he could have been in Camp Sheridan when Underhill built up this fantasy. Or perhaps the colonel had waited until Spur was gone before he laid his plans.

There was no problem following the trail of the horses. They had been on an arrow-like course for the Black Hills since they began, often going over small hills instead of around them through regular passes and along river beds.

As the light faded, Spur asked Kane how far ahead the troops were.

"Hey, I ain't no Indian. But I'd say maybe four hours."

"Are they walking or moving faster?"

"Walking, good cavalry procedure."

"Can you track them at night?"

"In stages. You give me a good lantern and let me stay a ways ahead. No, make that two lanterns and a holder."

Spur whistled and a trooper rode up with two kerosene lanterns.

"I'm a damngoogled hogwashing son-of-a-bitch! You planned this," said Buffalo Kane.

"Seen it done before. The trooper is Private Johnson. Kick your butt into a gallop and get as far up that trail as you can and when it gets dark, leave Johnson on the trail with the lantern. We'll find him. You move up the trail as fast as you can, on foot or horseback—your choice. Keep Johnson in sight. When you get on the trail, and Johnson waves the lantern that we have his position, let Johnson catch up to you. Keep it moving that way. Take ten men with you and use them as a connecting file, dropping one off wherever necessary to keep in contact with the man behind him. Let's see how far we can get."

By eleven o'clock that night Kane was stumped. They had come to a section that showed a jumble of tracks. Kane waited for Spur to ride up.

"I'd say they had a minor skirmish here, sir. Say maybe ten to twelve hostiles with a chase. I can't rightly tell, but could be the patrol split up into five, maybe six groups chasing the redskins."

"Major Rutherford, any suggestions?" Spur asked.

"Let's make camp here and wait. Put twenty lookouts around camp and bed down. If we keep going all night, these men won't be much good for fighting come morning."

"Agreed, Major. Pass the word. Fires are permitted if the men want them. We're in force—we don't care if the Sioux know we are here. In fact it might be good if they know we're coming."

A half hour later thirty small cooking campfires dotted the valley as the men brewed coffee and ate hardtack and salt pork.

Spur routed the troops out of their blankets a half hour before sunrise and had them fed and ready to march with the first glimmer of light. He had sent out scouts during the night in five different compass headings north and northwest. The first came riding back ten minutes after they began moving north.

"Found them, sir! Or what's left of them. Small valley about five miles north and to the left. Looks like a medium-sized Sioux hunting camp. I heard the firing with daylight and lit out. Can't tell for sure what happened, but the colonel and his men are in the camp and there must be a hundred or more braves around them. I heard lots of rifle fire from the Indian positions."

"You're positive it's the colonel?"

"Yes, sir. I saw that big white horse he rides. No missing him. Looked like he had been wounded."

"Lead the way, Corporal. Major, bring the troops."

They rode.

Spur wished they could cover the whole distance at a gallop, with the bugler playing the attack call all the way. But the bugler was with the colonel, and the sturdy army mounts weren't made to travel so far at such speed. They cantered for the first mile, then sent out scouts to the area and moved along at a steady four-mile-an-hour pace. With luck, they should reach the area in a little less than an hour. If the Sioux kept up the dawn attack, Spur hoped the colonel could hold out. When Buffalo Kane told Spur they were a mile from the site of the fighting, Spur took a dozen of the best marksmen and rode ahead at a gallop. They would punish their horses for the mile and cut down the time of the first response. It might help.

At the scout's suggestion they came to the position along the ridge that the Indians held. They hobbled their exhausted horses and worked up to where they could see the trap. It had been neatly sprung by the attacking Sioux. The Indians held high ground on both sides of the hunting camp, and were systematically picking off the blue clad troopers below.

Spur positioned his twelve men on a line along the top and downward slope of the ridge, and at his command they began firing at the Indians on the near side. The first volley cut down ten of the Indians before they knew their backs were exposed. Then the men fired at will and within five minutes the hostiles on the near slope had retreated into the heavier growth timber and vanished over the side. Spur drew his men back on the downslope and bunched them along the ridge, expecting a flanking movement. It came almost immediately. Twenty Sioux stormed out of the woods. Most carried bows and arrows, but a few had rifles. Spur's well positioned men cut the charge to ribbons and drove back the survivors.

After another ten minutes the main body of troopers stormed down the valley and charged up both sides of the slopes, driving the overpowered and outnumbered redskins back into the woods.

By the time Spur had found his horse and ridden down to the former Indian camp, the situation was secure. He stared around at the destruction of the hunting camp. Bales of dried meat had been ripped open and scattered. The one tipi had been burned. He found more than a dozen bodies, half of them women and children.

Spur dismounted and strode up to Lt. Colonel Underhill who sat on a stump as an enlisted medical attendant dressed his wounded right arm. Spur motioned the enlisted man to stand back. He waved the others out of earshot and turned to Underhill, fury building on his face.

"Just what the hell do you think you're doing here, Underhill?" he thundered.

"Killing hostiles, as per my orders, Colonel."

"You have no orders to attack women and

children? You have no orders to attack peaceful hunting camps! You're a disgrace to the uniform you wear! If you weren't wounded, I'd knock you down and strip off your rank."

Underhill paled. "I was acting under orders. They came when you were gone. Major Rutherford saw them."

"That's why we came to save your stinking hide. How many men did you lose?"

"I . . . I don't know."

Spur called to a sergeant and told him to get a count of casualties for each of the units.

"Colonel, consider yourself under arrest until I can bring formal charges against you." Spur spun around and marched off, too angry to talk further. The sergeant brought him the casualty figures. Colonel Underhill's unit had lost eight dead and twelve wounded out of his forty-man group. Major Rutherford's troops had lost one dead and six wounded.

"We're still counting the Indian dead, sir. There are eighteen dead in the camp—eight women, four children and six braves."

"Was there another officer with the colonel?"

"Yes, sir, Lt. Pauley."

"Tell him I want a word with him."

Spur walked upstream a ways, found a rock and sat on it, staring into the rippling chattering water. Lt. Pauley came up shortly and saluted.

"Pauley, what the hell happened?"

"The colonel ordered us out, mostly my company and a few others. He said he wanted forty men. Said he could whip half the Sioux nation with forty good cavalrymen. So we marched. Almost at dusk, we ran into a band of about fifteen Sioux, some kind of hunting party. We attacked them. They scattered and we never drew blood. By the time we got back together, our scouts had located this camp. We attacked just at sundown and took the camp. Then as it got dark, more than a hundred Sioux surrounded us and started shooting rifles and arrows. We took casualties, but held off the Sioux until daylight when they resumed the attack. Shortly after that a friendly force appeared on our left flank and fired at the Indians, pushing them off the ridge. Then . . ."

"I know the rest of it. Did Colonel Underhill *order* you and your men to kill the women and children?"

"Yes, sir. He said the only good Indian was a dead Indian. He specifically told us to kill every Sioux we found."

"Thank you, Lieutenant. I'll want your sworn testimony after we get back to camp. Bring in your dead. We'll take them back to Camp Sheridan for burial. I want Underhill to take full responsibility for all these deaths."

It took them two hours to regroup, find all the horses, and to pull out of the camp. Spur ordered no looting, no more burning or destruction.

"These people were trying to lay in their winter's food supply," he told the troops. "What has been done here will take years to undo. In fact it may never heal over—it may fester for generations."

The march back to Camp Sheridan took the rest of the day. It was a tired, silent column of troops that rode into camp just before mess call that evening.

One point Spur wanted cleared up: were any of the rifles the Indians had been using missing army weapons? The serial numbers of the captured rifles had been carefully noted. His men had found twelve

187

rifles in the hunting camp which had been used by the attacking force of Sioux who came after the camp had been taken. Spur summoned Cpl. Kramer with his list of rifles and carbine serial numbers.

Ten of the twelve weapons matched those lost, stolen or missing from the Camp armory.

"Two were from men listed as missing in action, six were the ones that simply vanished from the supply room, and the other two were still signed out by current troopers," the supply man reported.

Spur thanked him and sent him away.

Major Rutherford came in and gave Spur his report of the operation.

"Did I understand correctly what happened at that camp, Colonel? You put Colonel Underhill under arrest?"

"Yes. The record will show that it was for his own safety. He was delirious from his wound but still trying to lead his men. I'm sending him to Omaha on the first available wagon going to Sidney to the train. The colonel is suffering from disorientation due to his wound, and it has seriously affected his ability to command. We also have two badly wounded men, including Captain Casemore, who should be moved to a hospital. That will be part of our reasoning. After the colonel gets two days' rest, I want you to draw orders for him and send him to the hospital in Omaha. I'll sign them."

"But isn't that a little extreme?"

Spur looked sharply at Major Rutherford.

"Damn right! It was 'extreme' when he took forty men and slaughtered the Indians in that hunting camp. Before they died, those Sioux women and children were aware of exactly how 'extreme' the colonel could be. It was also extreme that this camp had to commit a hundred fifty men to go to his rescue. The dead troopers under his and my command also bear witness to how extreme the action was." Spur got up and paced the length of the major's office. "Hell, Rutherford, you *know* he isn't capable of command! When we get him back to Omaha, the medical men there will know it as well and pension him out. He'll be well taken care of for the rest of his life."

"And he'll be out of the way so he can't endanger any more of our men needlessly," the major admitted.

"Right. That leaves you in temporary command of this camp. I'll recommend that you be appointed to permanent camp commander. That also will look good on your record when you come up for promotion."

Major Rutherford's sergeant opened the door without knocking.

"Sirs, I think you better come with me. Buffalo Kane has just called out Lt. Pauley and is threatening to kill him!"

# CHAPTER EIGHTEEN

Spur and Major Rutherford dashed outside and saw a crowd gathered around the officers' quarters. There was a lot of hooting and yelling but when the troopers saw the officers they quieted.

Kane stood with his legs spread, his right hand near the .44 on his hip. Twenty feet down the sun-baked company street stood Lt. Wes Pauley, still in his sweat-stained clothes from the ride. He was bareheaded and he stared hard at Kane. There was a cluster of men against the buildings and another crowd in the parade ground.

Spur touched Major Rutherford's shoulder, motioning him to let Spur handle the situation.

Fifty feet from Kane's back, Spur called out, "Kane, you have two weeks left on your army contract. Is he worth it?"

"Damn right, Colonel! This bastard led the patrol that gunned down my family. I heard some men talking on this last patrol. They said the cold-blooded son-of-a-bitch ordered them to shoot. He told them there was six Sioux warriors in the shack getting ready to attack. The men said Pauley knew all the time just my wife was inside. Then he used his own rifle and murdered my wife and my two sons while they watched. They'll testify if I have to smash it out of them."

"You're drunk again, Kane," Lt. Pauley said. "Everybody knows you make up stories when you get drunk."

"Trooper Wilson and Corporal Montgomery know what happened."

Spur saw Lt. Pauley look up quickly.

"They won't say a word. It's all a lie! Sure, both men go on patrols with me—they're from my company. You're just bluffing again, Kane, you drunken bum!"

Kane fired a round that went between Lt. Pauley's feet. The officer jumped, his hand darted to his weapon on his right hip, but then he stopped and held both his hands in the air.

"You shoot me now, Kane, and it will be murder. I'm not even reaching for my gun."

"You killed her, you son-of-a-bitch! You shot her down in cold blood and then you shot my boys. You don't deserve to live!"

"They were just *Indians* for Christ's sake, Kane! We're people. They were *Indians!*"

Kane fired again. His bullet creased the officer's pants leg, narrowly missing his boot. Pauley paled with anger and fright. He looked up and saw Spur and Major Rutherford.

"Major, make his listen to reason! Make this crazy man put down his pistol! I didn't know the squaw was in the goddamn shack. Then she come running out bleeding. Christ, she was just an *Indian!*"

"You bastard!" Kane shouted. "Draw like a man, or I'm going to shoot you down like the rattlesnake you are!"

Spur touched the major's sleeve and turned away. Both officers walked slowly away from the scene. They would swear they hadn't seen a thing.

"Major, no . . ." Pauley screamed.

"On *three,* Pauley, you murderer! One . . . two . . . three!" Kane drew and aimed his weapon, but Pauley kept his hands over his head. Kane sighted in carefully and fired. The round sliced through an inch of Lt. Pauley's leg.

"Now, damn you, Pauley, you got one more chance. Draw or I'll kill you with your hands in the air!"

Pauley staggered back from the blow of the slug, but kept his feet. Blood poured from the wound and he looked at it and snarled, "You're an animal, Kane. Colonel McCoy wants you. Look!"

Pauley pointed behind Kane and the second the scout turned his head, Pauley drew and fired in one swift move. But Kane had only pretended to look. He dove to his left, protected his weapon as he rolled and came up firing. His .44 snapped off three shots so fast they thundered like one round, and all three slammed into Lt. Pauley's chest as he tried to get off another shot. His gun fired, but the lines of communication between Wes Pauley's brain and his hand had been severed. The big gun swung down to the ground. It went off once as Pauley slammed backward, carried by the force of the three heavy slugs in his chest which dumped him on his back, dead in the dusty street.

At the sound of the gunshot, Spur and Major Rutherford turned and walked back to the circle of men.

"It's all over, Kane," Spur called. "Lay down your gun. We'll have a hearing, but it will be a fair and honest one. Any enlisted men with evidence will testify, I'll guarantee that."

"It won't work, Colonel. I know the army. You officers will protect your own and I'll hang."

"I'll be running the show, and I promise you it will be fair," Spur assured him.

Kane stood up slowly. He tossed down his weapon which Spur realized was empty, and drew another six-gun from his belt, aiming it at McCoy across the space that separated them.

"Won't work, Colonel. I been there. I seen it all before. He was a fucking *officer!* We all know it. Better settle it right now."

Kane fired. The round hit the dirt between the two officers.

"Let's talk about this, Kane. You're not drunk now. You know what you're doing," Spur called.

Spur noticed that some men from the patrol hadn't been to their barracks yet and still had their rifles and pistols. Some raised their weapons now, looking at the officers.

Without warning Kane fired again. This round hit Major Rutherford in the leg, knocking him down. Before Spur could intervene, a dozen shots by the surrounding troopers blasted and Kane jolted again and again as the .45 rounds and heavier rifle slugs slammed into his body.

"Cease fire!" Spur bellowed and the deadly company street became quiet. Spur ran to Kane, who lay on his back, his neck and chest already a mass of blood. Kane blinked as Spur lifted his head out of the dirt.

"Thanks, Colonel," he whispered. "I got my man . . . Nothing else to live for . . . Got to see Walking Fawn and my boys." He winked, his face contorted with pain and he slumped against Spur, dead.

Spur pointed to the nearest trooper. "You! Run and get Doc Jones! *Move!*" Then he turned to the still gawking troops. "I want every man who fired his weapon to move over here and stand for inspection."

The men hesitated, then a group moved slowly to one side, grim-faced but confident. They had done nothing more than defend one of their officers. Nobody could fault them for that.

"The rest of you men are dismissed. Report to your barracks at once."

Spur watched the troopers leave, some pausing to stare at Buffalo Kane's bloody corpse.

Spur motioned to a sergeant to take down the names and units of the men who had fired, then dismissed them all. Doc Jones came walking up, looked at Kane first, grunted, then nodded at Major Rutherford who sat on the ground, in pain but not making a sound.

"Managed to get yourself shot up right here in camp, eh, Vern? Knew it would happen. You're too easy on the troops." The medic checked the leg wound, using a sharp little knife to slit his pants leg. "Yep, went in, decided to stay there," the doctor continued. "Legs don't like a chunk of lead. I got to dig it out. Got me some of that new-fangled chloroform—knock you out like a wooden mallet. You'll never feel a thing." The doctor called to two troopers to carry the major to the medical office.

Spur stood there a minute, looking down at Buffalo Kane's body. The will to live had vanished as soon as he had revenged his family's murder. Deep and abiding love was a powerful thing, to affect a man that way. The detail which was moving the bodies of the dead troopers to ready them for burial the next day, picked up the scout's body and took it away.

An hour later, Spur had eaten at the officers' table, and was sitting in his quarters. He was little farther along in nailing down the gunrunners than he had been a week ago. His only real suspect was all too obvious—no one in his right mind would arrange for the sale of the guns, then volunteer to lead the escort that rode out to ensure the weapons' safe delivery into Camp Sheridan.

Or would he? Would it seem to be so obvious as to be ludicrous, and therefore effective? Spur thought about it. There had been no connecting file to contact the other unit so the main parties could meet. No scouts had pointed the right direction. And the escort's route was eight miles off course.

The more he thought of it, the more plausible it became. Lt. Imhoff was a cocky bastard, just the kind to try to make a big deal any way he could. With all that gold in the Black Hills, the kind of payment was obvious, too. Yes, the personality fit. Imhoff had been in the army only a short time. He bragged about how he had bribed a senator to get a spot on active duty. Imhoff could be the man. But how to smoke him out?

If Imhoff had been stealing rifles from supply and selling them a few at a time to the Indians, he must have hidden the payment somewhere, perhaps in his quarters. He was unmarried and would have quarters similar to Spur's. An unofficial inspection of the officer's room might prove helpful. Spur looked down the housing chart he had been provided with the first day and found Imhoff's quarters. The newer men were farthest from the center of the camp. Imhoff was second to the end of the officers' units. Spur realized that the sun had set and his room was dark. Good.

He slipped out the back door and walked down to the next to last building. There was no light. Imhoff might have been asked out for dinner.

On the way back to his quarters, Spur went around to the front of the buildings and stopped at the dispensary. The lights were on and he heard voices behind a door. He opened it and found Doc Jones washing his hands. An enlisted man was wrapping a bandage around the major's thigh.

"Got the damn thing. Deep in there beside the bone. Thank God for chloroform. Would have taken six men to hold Vern down without it. A real Godsend," the doctor muttered.

"He'll be back on duty?" Spur asked.

"In a week he'll be walking. Vern is strong as an ox. No lasting damage, but he'll have one hell of a scar."

The major wasn't moving.

"He still unconscious?"

"Yep. Great, isn't it? He'll be coming around in five minutes or so. Right now I got to get to dinner.

Felicia is holding it for me and making polite conversation with that blowhard Imhoff. Never liked him too much. I got to wait until Vern comes back to his senses, then I'm gone."

"Thanks, Doc, you do good work." Spur left the hospital and walked back to his quarters. Again he went through the back door and to Lt. Imhoff's rear entrance. He knocked, got no response and tried the door. Locked. Spur used his key and was not surprised to find that it fit. There were only two types of long skeleton keys that fit the keyhole locks. He turned the key and stepped into the blackness of the room.

Spur barred the front door, then hung a blanket over the front window and lit a small candle. He started searching the most obvious hiding spots—under the bunk, in the bottom of a wooden foot locker. Finding nothing, he moved to the shelf in a small closet and then to a dresser. In the bottom drawer under a spare army blanket he found it. Three rawhide pouches. Spur opened one and looked inside. Gold, mostly in small jagged chunks. Not nuggets, long washed by a stream, or gold dust, but chunks! He pocketed three of the pieces of gold, put everything back exactly the way it had been, and removed the blanket from the window. He heard voices outside the door and, quickly unbolting it, hurried out the rear entrance. Just as he locked the back door, he heard the front one open.

Back in his room, Spur knew the evidence was circumstantial, but it was all he had, and for him it was enough. First he would have to force Imhoff to admit his complicity, then figure out how to get the rifles back. He would play it by ear. A hideout gun might come in handy. He took a small .22 caliber derringer, loaded it and pushed it down the inside of his boot. Now for a long talk with Lt. Imhoff.

As he walked the hundred yards to Imhoff's room, Spur decided it might be good strategy to lead Imhoff on, ask for a share of the gold. It might get an interesting reaction.

Spur would try the back door approach. He knocked on the panel and waited. Spur heard movement inside, and a few seconds later a voice called, "Yes, who is it?"

"A friend, Imhoff. I need to talk to you."

"McCoy? Colonel McCoy?"

"Easy, we don't need a lot of names shouted around."

"I was in bed. Just a minute—let me get my pants on."

After what Spur guessed were two minutes, the door unlocked and opened. Imhoff stared out. "It *is* you. What's so damned important it couldn't wait until morning?"

"I'll tell you inside. I feel exposed out here."

Imhoff grinned in the half light. "That sounds ominous. Come in, Colonel, come in."

One lamp burned in the room, but it was turned low. The bed was mussed, blankets turned back. Clothes lay around the room. Spur leaned against the back door, crossed his arms and stared at Imhoff.

"How long have you been in the army?"

"Counting West Point, four and a half years, sir."

"And right now you're thinking that I'm totally stupid, right? You're laughing behind my back every chance you get. Well, Imhoff, I'll say this.

198

You covered your tracks well, right up to volunteering for that escort. That was the dumb part. Damn, at first I didn't even consider you! Too obvious. But you counted on that. When is the final payment—tonight? I should have known that a bullshitter like you would be the one. Gladhander, life of the party, and about as amoral as they come. How much did you get for the first ten rifles, Imhoff? Maybe fifteen pounds of gold? Let's see—fifteen pounds at twenty dollars and sixty-seven cents an ounce is about five thousand dollars. Not bad for a start."

"Colonel, you're talking right out your asshole, you know that? I don't understand a word you're saying."

"What about the three rawhide sacks of gold in your bottom dresser drawer?"

Imhoff winced. His eyes narrowed and he brought a .44 pistol from behind his back.

"I'll be damned, you must be smarter than we figured. The escort did it, I guess. It was a risk I had to take. You see, I'm new here and nobody told me about the escort going out to meet the supply wagons. A minor slipup, but I covered it."

"You *thought* you covered it."

"They got the rifles, didn't they?"

"They did. And a lot of troopers are going to die because of those weapons and ammunition."

"But you're not in much of a position to do anything about it, are you, Colonel?"

"Depends how much you know about me. You think I'd come in here blind, bluffing, and without an ace in the hole?"

"What do you mean?"

"I've got a complete report on you, a sample of

the gold, the whole story spelled out. It's hidden deep in the camp files, but in a spot that would be first to be searched if anything 'unfortunate' happened to me. I've told one sergeant on base what to do if I wake up some morning and find myself dead."

"So you're covered. You're still dead. You wouldn't bet everything on that. You've got more."

"True, lots more. What it all boils down to, Lieutenant, is that I didn't get to be a colonel by following the book. I picked you out as a man a lot like me that first day. What I'm saying is, if you and I can strike the right bargain, we both could go on living, and we both could wind up so filthy rich we would never have to see the inside of any army post again."

"Partners? You joking? I've done all the work."

"But I'll be taking the big risk. I'll be covering for you officially. I'm the only one who can take suspicion off you and let you resign gracefully and not have U.S. government agents chasing you for the next sixty years."

"Hell, I don't know . . . I need some time."

Spur saw motion from the corner of his eye and turned. Felicia Jones lifted up from the space between the wall and the bed. She was naked. She sat casually on the edge of the bed, smiling.

"Colonel, I think you're exactly right. We *do* need someone on the inside. Come over here and sit beside me and let's discuss this situation on a more personal basis." She looked at Imhoff. "Omer, you go down and check out Colonel McCoy's quarters. See what you can find. He and I will confer here, and you *know* this is the kind of convincing I do best!"

# CHAPTER NINETEEN

When Felicia was sure that Imhoff had left, she pulled Spur down beside her, then kissed him.

"Now sweet Spur, we're going to have a conference." She began undressing him. "First, I like the idea of your joining us. We do need someone inside, and I've been worried about your effect on us ever since you came. You're too smart for our good. But a three-way split on, say, a hundred thousand dollars worth of gold isn't bad. We've got two powder kegs of raw chunk gold coming, like that you saw in the dresser. And when we get this we'll know where it is, *exactly*. What would you say to going back in with a twenty-man civilian guard and bringing out a *wagon-load* of gold!"

Felicia had his shirt off and was unbuttoning his fly. Spur couldn't stop the hot blood from rushing into his crotch and his manhood stood up stiff and ready. Felicia laughed softly, then grabbed him.

"Let's talk about the gold," Spur said.

She laughed and kissed his erection. "You must

be joking! The lady wants to be loved. She wants to lie down and have you pump her, and you're talking about gold?"

Spur looked at her lovely young body, so sleek, so smooth, breasts so round and full, so chalky white and throbbing as her nipples filled and lifted. Her flowing hair shading one pretty eye, teasing him. Spur reached out and touched her flat little belly and the thatch below, and he knew he wasn't going to talk about gold for a while.

"Oh, yes, now that's better, big Spur man. You can spur me anytime you want to!" She moved to her hands and knees on the bed and grinned at him. "Dinner time," she said and Spur growled and pushed his head under her and lay on his back, her delightful breast teasing him, dipping low enough for him to lick, then to suck a moment before lifting and the other one swinging in, moving in and out like a dance routine.

Spur reached to her crotch and found it wet and ready. His mouth sucked on her ripe hanging fruit as his finger found the small trigger just over her slit and he played the hard node back and forth like a guitar.

"Don't do that, I'm not ready yet. No! Oh, God but that feels delicious. Not yet, I want you inside me!" She crooned as she arched over him, losing her balance and falling on top of him, quivering for a full minute, until she tapered off and made soft purring sounds. She rested a minute, then was back on her knees.

"Christ, but you are good! Nobody makes me explode that way so quick. How do you do it?"

He laughed and bit her breasts and she urged him

on. His hand found her crotch again and she groaned.

"Your turn, sweetheart, your turn. You ever play doggie? Can you do the doggie?"

Spur sat up and moved behind her where she still crouched on her hands and knees. He positioned himself and then edged into her, making her cry out with joy.

"So different! God, but that feels different! What are you *doing* back there?" She looked over her shoulder, laughing in a delighted way that encouraged him to continue.

He pushed deeper until she had consumed him and then leaned over her back, caught one of her breasts in each hand and massaged them.

"If I was a queen, I would keep you around just to fuck me. You're so *good*. You know more good places and positions and more *wonderful* little tricks!"

Somebody knocked on the back door.

"No, Goddamnit!" she screeched. "Get out of here, Omer. Go diddle yourself somewhere. Come back in an hour."

Spur laughed. "What if that wasn't Omer?"

"Then the biddies will have lots to gossip about tomorrow. Shut up and fuck."

Spur did. There was something about this kneeling position that always made him feel like an animal in season. It was best for his fifth or sixth time, usually not the first, but there was no turning back now—not that he wanted to.

His mind exploded and his body followed, jolting forward, almost pushing Felicia flat. She was moaning and shuddering at the same time, crying out so loudly that he was sure she'd wake the entire camp.

Then both of them collapsed on the bed and neither could speak as they lay there panting. Ten minutes later they still lay side by side on the bed. His hand played with her breasts.

"What happened to the payoff for the rifles?" he asked.

"It's right on schedule. We meet our guide at a lightning-struck snag out on the river, and he takes us into Sioux country. We pick up the two kegs of gold packed on Indian ponies and ride out."

"Why do you need me?"

"Officially, you can grease the rough spots. I'll be going out on the next wagon to Sidney to catch the train. Father knows I'm leaving. He can get by. But Imhoff needs to resign with no suspicion."

"And that's where I come in. You want me to sell out my career for thirty thousand dollars?"

"That alone is a fortune. You must make eighty, maybe ninety-five dollars a month, maybe even a hundred. Thirty thousand dollars in twenty years' army pay! And this is just the beginning. You've heard of *Rio del Oro?*"

"Yes—a fantasy. Some Spanish padre's dream."

"No dream, reality! It exists in there somewhere —a stretch of stream that runs across solid gold. Not quartz or dust, but solid gold like you saw in those bags. Think what we could do with a *ton* of gold!"

"A lot of money, granted, but. . . ."

"Not a *lot* of money, a huge, unthinkable sum! It would be almost seven hundred thousand dollars! Just one run with a good wagon, a dozen dray horses and about twenty men for protection."

"Protection from the army or the Indians?"

"The army wouldn't even know we were around. The Indians might."

"I heard that Chief Crazy Eyes can bring together over three thousand Sioux warriors. How can we go in with twenty rifles?"

"In the first place, each man will have two Sharps 12-shot repeaters. That's twenty-four shots before reloading. And we go in during the worst weather we can find, preferably rain. We don't let any scout or lookout who sees us get back to the tribe."

"You'll be along?"

"Damn right! I've been practicing. I can use a rifle better than half the troopers in camp."

"Do we get a look at this river of gold at payoff time?"

"That's the plan. We get as close to it as we can, scout out a route, and judge what kind of alert system the Indians have around it. From what I hear, it's only about two hundred yards long, up in the hills somewhere. One small problem may be that the Sioux consider it to be hallowed ground, about as sacred as it can get except for the chief's burial cave. But the injuns won't even know we're in there. We'll slip in and out with a ton of pure gold, ready for market!"

"If this *Rio del Oro* is really there, how come nobody has charged in there before and taken the gold?"

"I'll spell it out for you. S-I-O-U-X. The big bad Sioux don't want anybody to know about it. But I've got me two specialists in fighting the Sioux. How can we go wrong?"

Spur pushed her breasts together, admiring her

cleavage.

"How can we go wrong? About a thousand ways. You've got a dozen things that have to mesh together *right*. The weather, the time, hunting parties, the buffalo. What about your own men? Twenty guards could mutiny and take over the wagon of gold, reward us with a bullet in the head and jump their wages from two hundred for the week's work into thirty thousand dollars each! An operation like this has a thousand problems."

"Look, you big idiot, I never said it would be easy. I said we can *do* it!"

She sat up and began pulling on her clothes which she gathered from the floor beside the bed. "I said we needed you, not that we couldn't get along without you. You could still have an accident and wind up stiff in a pine box by morning."

"And by noon both you and Imhoff would be in the guard house."

"I think that's a bluff." She stepped into a pair of ruffled drawers. Spur enjoyed watching her. When she finished, he dressed. He forgot and pushed his right foot into his boot. He had edged the derringer down there as he undressed so Felicia hadn't seen it. Now he pulled it out and put it in place again without her noticing.

She stood with her hands on her hips. The blouse pulled tightly across her breasts and Spur enjoyed the view.

"All right, I've decided. I want you to come along tonight on our payoff pickup. I don't like the three-way split, so we'll make it two way and lose Lt. Imhoff somewhere beyond Sioux country."

"That's probably what he's expecting by now," Spur said.

"We won't give him any reason to think that. I'll be mean and nasty to you the rest of the night and on the trip. It'll all be an act, of course. Then we take care of Imhoff when we're well out of Sioux country and don't need him anymore."

"And how do I know that you won't tell Imhoff the same thing about me?"

"Oh, no, sweet Spur. I'd never do that. You fuck too good!" She stood in front of him, went to her knees and kissed his fly and crotch a dozen times. "I love this big one too much to kill him, ever!"

Spur caught her by both arms and lifted her up.

"Sounds reasonable and logical to me. When do we leave?"

"Midnight. That will give us time to get in touch with our contact and to get well away from the fort before we're missed."

"What excuse do we give?"

"You'll leave a note on your door that you've discovered a possible location of the rifles, and will be back in a week. You're taking Lt. Imhoff with you. I'll tell Father I'm on a secret mission and he has to cover for me for the next week. Then I'll be back. He'll do it."

"You've thought it all out. What about supplies? We still need to eat."

She pulled two army storage bags out from under Lt. Imhoff's bed. "Filled with enough food to last us for a month. Even some tinned goods in there. We've been buying it a little at a time for a month."

"You *do* plan ahead. Let me go get into some

207

civilian clothes. I'd guess that's what we'll be wearing so we don't rile the Sioux any more than necessary?"

"Yes. And bring that Spencer with you. We shouldn't need it, but you never can tell about the Sioux. Come back here at midnight."

Spur ducked out the back door and walked quickly to his own quarters' rear entrance. It was open. Lt. Imhoff sat there with a six-gun in his hand and it was pointed right at Spur.

"What the hell you doing with my woman?" he snarled.

"Imhoff, that kind is everybody's woman. Don't waste your time with her. You're a bigger boy than that."

Imhoff scowled, swore, then jammed the pistol back in his belt.

"Shit, she spreads her legs for anybody. Hell, maybe you're right. When we get this gold, I'm riding out. I'll leave the bitch for good."

Spur nodded agreement. "I'm going along."

Imhoff nodded, some of his good humor returning. "Hell, it might come in handy to have another gun along on this run after all. I'm not a hundred percent convinced, but we'll play the hand and see what happens. Colonel, I still don't trust your ass. And, remember, when we're both in civilian clothes, them eagles on your shoulder don't mean shit!"

They left the post shortly after midnight. Spur and Imhoff had each carried one of the supply sacks to the stables. The guard there was given a two dollar gold piece and they packed up and took one extra saddled horse—for emergencies, they told the stable guard.

As arranged, Felicia met them outside the gate near the river. She wore a split riding skirt and Spur was not surprised to see her riding astride as she took command of the whole operation. It was going to be an interesting journey.

At the same jagged, dead cottonwood tree where Imhoff had met the Sioux warrior before, they waited. The brave rode up with two others and after a brief conversation conducted chiefly in sign language, the Indians led the way north. Spur watched Felicia eyeing the braves, wondering if she would try to lure them into her blankets before the trip was over. The braves did not even look at her.

Two days later they were in the foothills. Nothing eventful had happened on the trip. Felicia had remained in her own blankets, tired after each day's long ride. The morning of the third day found them high in the Black Hills. Spur memorized the route and noted that they had turned west early and then north. He estimated they were thirty miles from where he had seen the first hunting camp with Chitsa as his guide. He wondered where she was now. At last report, she had ridden into the Nebraska plains and no one had seen or heard from her since.

High on a ridge overlooking a gentle valley where the glistening trace of a small stream could be seen, the three Sioux braves stopped. With sign language, the Indians indicated the three whites should dismount and wait. Each of the braves carried a new Sharps carbine, the type that had been on the shipment from Omaha. The Sioux had apparently put their new weapons to use quickly.

"I don't like it," Imhoff said, staring at the backs

of the Sioux as they worked their way down a steep trail toward the valley below. "I say we follow the bastards and get the gold and leave."

"You say you want to get an arrow or a .52 caliber slug in your brain," Spur replied. "We're in Sioux territory. We play the game their way or they take away your chips and replace them with our own scalplocks."

"He's right, Omer, and you know it. So sit down and relax."

"I'll relax with you, pretty tit," Imhoff said.

Felicia scowled. "I don't like that kind of talk when I'm not in the mood. And I'm not." She forced a smile. "Omer, once we have the gold, and we're on our way out of here, all three of us will have a party."

"Hell, I'm not much on sharing," Imhoff grumbled. "Damn!"

They waited for one hour, then another. Spur was watching the progress of the horses below. They had moved to the center of the valley where the little stream widened somewhat. The braves stayed there for some time and then moved back up the hill, leading two pack animals. Imhoff lifted his binoculars.

"Damn, they're finally heading back."

"Look!" Spur said. The sun had moved to a point where it shone directly into the center of the small stream and the light bounced off in a direct reflection that was blinding.

"The *Rio del Oro*," Felicia breathed softly.

"God, it's got to be the damn gold stretch!" Imhoff shouted.

"Either that, or they put a lot of mirrors in the river bed to fool us," Felicia said.

"If that is holy ground down there, I'm surprised they let us come this far so we could see it," Spur said. "I'd bet they will have a show of force to remind us how strong the Sioux are in this area, and as a warning not to come back."

"Back, hell. I'm not leaving until I can walk on that gold river bottom!" Imhoff declared.

"Don't mention it to the Sioux," Spur shot back. "Look, I know more about the Sioux than both of you. We do exactly what they tell us. We take the gold and we get our asses out of here. Imhoff, if you want to come back later, that's up to you. But, I'll shoot you down on the spot if you turn and ride down that trail into the valley while the Sioux are watching."

"Hell, Colonel, don't get your eagles shitting all over your shoulder. I ain't that dumb. I don't want to taste those Sioux arrowheads or their Sharps lead. You worry about your own ass, and I'll take care of mine."

Spur ignored him and watched the pack animals coming slowly up the hill. It took the Indian pack ponies a half hour to come up the steep trail even when led by the Sioux braves. At the top, the Indian said something and motioned to the ex-army powder kegs. The tops had been broken out and they sat upright on the back of the pack horse, tied down on four sides. Spur estimated the kegs must weigh a hundred and fifty pounds each.

Imhoff went forward, checked out the gold, tried to lift the kegs to test their weight, then nodded.

"Looks fine to me, chief," Imhoff said to the Indian, then made some sign Spur had never seen before. The brave responded with other signs, and at last pointed into the valley, shook his head and held up both hands as if holding the whites back.

"Sure, chief. We understand. We won't set foot in the valley of the Great Spirit. Yeah, sure. Thanks for the gold. You ever want any more good Sharps carbines, you give me a smoke signal."

The Indians turned and trotted down the hill, never looking back.

"Let's get out of here," Spur said. He caught the rawhide lead rope of one of the pack ponies and mounted his bay. The others mounted as well and soon they were working their way south.

"You'll notice the Sioux did not give us an escort on the return trip," Spur observed.

"I wondered about that," Felicia admitted.

Imhoff handed the lead on his pack pony to Felicia.

"You two go on ahead, I'll catch up with you. I have to go have a look at that river of gold. I at least want to say I saw it, *touched* it."

"No!" Felicia shouted, her voice enraged. "You go back there and they'll find you and kill you. We're riding south!"

Imhoff rode up to her and glared down. "Little bitch, you don't have any hold over me anymore. I've got the gold, and I'll do any damn thing I want to." He wheeled and rode at a right angle to them, moving to a different spot along the ridge to make his descent into the valley.

Felicia drew the .44 from her saddle, but Spur's hand closed over it before she could fire.

"You fire one shot and half the Sioux nation will be down on us. There's not a hell of a lot we can do to stop him. Maybe it's all for the best. He wants his reward for selling guns to the Sioux. Maybe the Sioux themselves will provide it."

They rode south another mile, hid the horses in a ravine with heavy brush over and tied them well, then walked back up to the ridgeline.

Both wormed their way to the very top and peered down into the valley. Spur took out his binoculars and sectioned the lush green mile-long valley. At last he saw movement down the near side of the slope. It was Imhoff, moving slowly from tree to tree. Spur checked but saw no Indians in the area. He showed Felicia.

"The fool might just make it yet, if the Sioux believed that we would not go down there. But somehow I doubt that."

"The Sioux are learning the ways of the white man—trust no one," Felicia said.

All they could do was watch. She moved up beside him.

"I know I *said* we should let the Sioux have Imhoff, but I don't think I could have done it. Now he's made the move himself." She pressed against Spur and he put his arm around her.

"Have you ever seen a man die, Felicia?"

Her eyes widened and she shook her head.

"It's not pretty. All we can do is wait and see what happens. If they catch him, they will kill him, there is no doubt about that. The big question is, will they then come after us for letting him go back and violate their sacred lands?"

"You think the Sioux . . ."

"Yes, without doubt. They have acted as men of honor, fulfilling their bargain. Now if the white man does not keep his bargain, which includes not going into the valley, then all bets are off. It's open warfare—kill or be killed. And the Sioux will have one hell of an advantage."

"Maybe we should leave now?" she said.

"An extra ten minutes or half hour wouldn't matter. It will be better to know than to run scared and wonder what happened to Imhoff."

"You're a gambler. What are the odds?"

"Of being caught down there? At least a thousand to one, and not in Imhoff's favor. If he's seen and caught, his chances of getting away are a million to one. And it won't be pretty."

Spur used the binoculars again, checking the far slope beyond the river. He winced, then, at last put down the glasses. He turned Felicia's pretty face to him and kissed her lips.

"Do you want to leave now?" he asked.

She frowned and watched him intently. "You saw something! What did you see? Sioux?"

"The Sioux may be mighty warriors, but they aren't in the same class with the Chiricahua Apache. So far I've seen five Sioux warriors who are supposed to be hidden in the brush and grass. All of them are moving slightly, just enough to give away their position. If I can spot five, there may well be a hundred. But five is plenty to cut Imhoff into buffalo jerky."

"My God! Let's warn him!"

Spur used the glasses again. Imhoff was at the stream, jumping up and down, and probably shouting with rapture, but Spur couldn't hear him. Imhoff walked in the stream, then sat down on the bottom which evidently was little more than a foot under the surface.

A bullet slammed into the water beside Imhoff. He jumped up and ran for the bank where he had left his rifle. A dozen rounds struck on and around the rifle. Imhoff stood immobile.

A long, low wailing call echoed through the valley and the Sioux warriors stood. They had nearly circled the valley.

"My God, look at that!" Felicia said softly.

"I'd say about two hundred Sioux braves, all armed with rifle, bow and arrow or spear. Lt. Imhoff is in an unenviable situation."

"Don't joke about it!"

"There's nothing we can do to help him. Let's go."

"No, no! We must be sure."

They waited. The Indians closed in slowly, firing only at his rifle when he made a move toward it. He held his hands over his head, then suddenly went for his pistol and fired three times, wounding the closest Indian, but an arrow slashed through his right wrist and knocked the weapon from his hand. The braves closed in then and Imhoff faced them, laughing.

"Why haven't they ended it?" Felicia asked.

"A quick death is seldom the Indian way for a captive. We should leave."

"No!"

They watched as three braves ran from the woods with three long poles. Spur shook his head. He knew what was coming. The Sioux moved quickly then. The poles were arranged in a triangle and the tops tied together. Imhoff was tied by the feet and hung from the center of the poles. His hands were tied behind him.

"Why are they doing that?" Felicia asked.

Spur just shook his head.

A brave moved in with hands full of something. They couldn't see what it was for sure. Spur knew but wouldn't say. Soon a small trail of smoke arose as a fire began to burn.

When the light breeze was right they could hear Imhoff screaming, but still Felicia wouldn't leave.

"Burning him at the stake!" she asked. Spur saw that she was crying softly.

"No. Worse than that, much worse."

Felicia bit her lip. "I want to stay."

The fire at first was small. Lt. Imhoff's head was six feet from the fire. Gradually he was lowered by a strong rawhide rope until the fire made him squirm and shout.

Spur had heard that this execution ritual sometimes took as long as four hours, depending on the skill and patience of the Indian who kept the fire burning at precisely the correct level.

The valley was quiet except for Imhoff's tortured, wailing scream that came floating on the breeze now and then. His hair had burned away.

"Is he . . . is he dead yet?" Felicia asked, her face turned away.

"No. They make it last a long time." Spur had heard of the torture, of how the victim would scream and fight. His hair might burn off quickly and he would be in shock, but alive. His scalp would blister and then the rope would lower him another foot toward the flames. Soon the blood in his brain would boil. Blood vessels would rupture and the victim would die in a screaming intolerable white-hot agony of pain.

But the ceremony would still continue. The head

would continue to be lowered until at last the victim's skull would explode and the game would be over.

Spur used the binoculars again. Lt. Imhoff's head was black. Fluid ran from one ear. The rope slipped another two inches, moving his blackened skull closer to the searing heat.

Spur put the glasses away, picked up Felicia Jones and carried her down the hill toward their horses. They might have an hour's head start if they were lucky.

When they reached their mounts, Spur used his knife and cut the thongs holding the two powder kegs of gold, carried them to the base of a huge pine tree with two tops, and covered them with pine needles, branches and fallen limbs. He made it look as natural as possible.

Felicia sat staring at him in wonder.

"Our gold . . ." she whimpered.

"No gold. We're trying to save our scalps. Carrying that weight, the horses would never have a chance. Now we can ride the Indian ponies until they drop, then put the saddles back on our regular mounts and keep riding. With luck we can be ten miles away before the Sioux start pursuing us."

"We must take the gold . . ."

"We must save our hides!" He had taken her saddle off and now cinched it in place on the Indian pony. He tied the reins of her army mount to the saddle and boosted her up. His own mounts were ready and they rode, Spur in the lead, angling down the slope to the edge of the valley. It didn't matter who saw them now. He looked back and saw Felicia keeping up with him. She was a good rider and that

217

might make the difference. The Indian ponies were fast and sure-footed. Spur sent them galloping across the short valley, up the ridge and over it. Down the other side he let them rest at a fast walk, and when they reached the next valley, he spurred them back to a hard run. Spur figured fifteen miles for the tough little horses. Then they would refuse to run, having a natural instinct when to stop before they killed themselves.

Felicia pulled up beside him.

"Was he dead? Did you *see* Lt. Imhoff die?"

"Yes. His hair burned off his skull . . ."

Felicia turned away. "I'm coming back for the gold. Someday I'm coming back and I'll dig it up. I'll remember exactly where it is. I'm coming back."

Spur rode on silently, concentrating on finding the best route. He had consciously headed south, knowing that they had to work eastward as well, but that a southerly route should take them out of Sioux country faster.

They had been riding for two hours. The Indian ponies were exhausted. They rode up to the brow of a hill and when Spur looked over it he saw a large Sioux hunting camp. He reined back and held up a hand to stop Felicia.

"Trouble." He turned and they rode along the far side of the ridge for half a mile. When he looked over the ridge he found more of the camp. It must be a permanent village of some sort. Should they wait until night? The Indian mounts were winded.

Spur headed east again, moving into a small valley, running just inside the woods line, and noticing that the timber were thinning. Ahead there would be only prairie, grasslands with no means of concealment. Spur went to the top of the next ridge and looked below. More Indians. A sea of tipis spread out in a large valley with a sizable stream running through the center. They were in the middle of a Sioux encampment—some kind of a gathering, a powwow maybe.

Felicia came up on Spur's right. She was shaking. "Spur, look, an Indian!"

Spur drew his six-gun as he spun to his left. An Indian girl on a horse burst from some trees and rode straight for them. A glance at the girl's face made Spur smile and put his pistol away. Felicia was clawing for her weapon.

"No," Spur said firmly. "Felicia, you know Chitsa from Camp Sheridan."

"Oh. Can she help us?"

"Chitsa, how long have you been following us? Never mind, can you get us out of this trap?" Spur asked.

She smiled. "And hello to you too, Spur McCoy. Yes, I can get you out. Follow me, and be as quiet as possible."

For the next hour they rode cautiously, hid in brush, then rode like the wind through a valley and over another ridge. When they were on the down slope Chitsa pulled her Indian pony to a walk and motioned for Spur to ride beside her.

"To answer your first question, I have followed you since you left Camp Sheridan four days ago. I saw your meeting with the three Sioux braves, and I got close enough to see the *Rio del Oro*. But I was not foolish enough to let the Sioux see me as Lt. Imhoff did. May God rest his soul."

"Will the Sioux follow us?"

"Will the sun come up in the morning?"

"How far behind us are they?"

"Close enough for you to change horses. We'll be in the grasslands in a few more hours, when the army mount's stamina should be of good use."

"We have a chance then?"

"You saved your scalp when you left the gold. If you had brought it with you, you would both have been scalped two hours ago. Let's ride."

Near dusk that day they saw twenty Sioux horsemen that Chitsa said were the ones following them.

They rode all night, using the darkness to good advantage and when the sun came up they had less than a day's ride to make Camp Sheridan. Felicia, worn out, nearly fell out of her saddle twice. They stopped and Chitsa stood watch while the other two slept for a while, then she roused them and they rode hard for two hours, let the horses walk for an hour and rode hard again.

Just before darkness they rode into Camp Sheridan, and within minutes the entire population came out to welcome them.

# CHAPTER TWENTY

Spur sat in the officers' mess, eating. He had never been so hungry, even though he hadn't thought about food during the past three days. It had been butchering day at Camp Sheridan and Spur finished his second two-pound steak with mashed potatoes, thick brown gravy and butter fried parsnips. At last he pushed the plate back.

Major Rutherford chuckled where he straddled a chair leaning on the back, his chin resting on his folded forearms.

Spur had filled him on most of the affair as he ate.

"So Imhoff was the gunrunner all along. I never thought he might be the one."

"Gold does strange things to men—and women."

"That presents a problem. Nobody else knows how involved Felicia was. If we don't charge her, it will blow over."

"She will be put on a train somewhere. She wants to get away from here, I understand."

"We'll work it out. Doc is crushed. He had no idea

she was so eager to leave. I've ordered a wagon to take Colonel Underhill and his family to Sidney, and thence to Omaha." Major Rutherford grinned. "I lied a little bit, cleaning up Underhill's record. And knowing Underhill, he'll make out all right. His wound isn't that bad but they'll figure out quickly that he is in no mental state to command."

"What about Imhoff?"

"I'll take my cue from you. You'll write a report. I'll include it with mine. I'd just as soon tell it like it happened. We don't owe Imhoff a thing."

Spur left the table and they walked down the line of officers' quarters.

"Let's take a detour," Spur said. They went to Lt. Imhoff's room and Spur used the Major's pass key. Inside they lit a lamp and Spur looked in the bottom dresser drawer. The three bags of gold were still there. He picked them up and blew out the lamp.

"Let's go to your office for a talk," Spur said.

A half hour later they had reached an agreement. There had never been such a thing as the *Rio del Oro*. The fifteen pounds of pure gold Spur carried did not exist. He would turn it over to the mint without a clue where it originated.

"If the gold story got out, you'd have five thousand miners in here before winter," Spur said. "And the Sioux would probably kill all of them. You don't have enough men to protect everyone. Let's hold off the Black Hills gold rush as long as we can."

"You actually didn't see this river of gold, then?"

"I saw a stream maybe fifteen feet wide, and a flash of sunlight off something in the water. But I didn't see a gold-lined stream bed. Imhoff did and you know what happened to him. Major, that about wraps me up here. Right now I better find my bunk before I fall asleep in your chair."

"You'll be moving out soon, Colonel?"

"Yes, I came here strictly to find the gunrunners and stop them. As you've no doubt figured out, that doesn't sound much like a regular army job, and it isn't. Those eagles of mine are what you might call temporary rank."

"And I imagine I'm not supposed to ask any questions," the major said.

"Ask, but I won't answer. Yes, I'll be leaving as soon as I get some sleep. Probably the day after tomorrow. How is Casselberry doing?"

"Both Casselberrys are doing fine. Janet has been totally accepted into society, and Neil is working his balls off with his company." Major Rutherford paused. "Just for my own information, Janet *had* been caught by the Sioux, hadn't she?"

"Yes. Two of them. One got away, one didn't."

"I figured that. Now why don't you get some shut-eye?"

Two days later Spur McCoy in civilian clothes mounted his bay in front of the Camp Sheridan headquarters. Felicia Jones would be on the wagon to Sidney within the week. She had been pointedly excluded from the camp's social activities. Chitsa would be going to Omaha with the Underhills. Spur shook the major's hand one last time, returned his salute and rode out the south gate on the wagon track through the prairie. It would be an easy ride, and Spur looked forward to it.

He was barely an hour away from the post when he heard hoofbeats behind him on the sod. He turned and saw someone riding hard toward him—a girl with long black braids flying behind her. She rode up until her leg touched his. Chitsa had on a white blouse and a pair of cut down army pants. She looked beautiful.

"I decided to go for a ride. Mind if I tag along with you? I'll meet the Underhills in Sidney."

"I'm delighted!" He leaned over and kissed her soft, parted lips. "I have a lot of thank-you's to say to you for saving my scalp."

"That's what good friends are for," she said softly.

He took her hand, suddenly wanting to touch her. Spur smiled and she smiled back. She would be his love slave for three whole days.

Spur McCoy, United States Secret Agent, knew he had the best job in the world. And for the next few days he and Chitsa would be on the trail together. They would camp early, make a fire, eat and then enjoy a love-filled night.

Spur grinned. Damn, this was the life!